The Present Past

Leonard St. Clair Ross

The Present Past

Cover Design: Dan Ross

ISBN - 9781626130739

Library of Congress Control Number - 2016943692

Published by ATBOSH Media ltd.

Cleveland, Ohio, USA

http://www.atbosh.com

Foreword

Traditionally, the "about the author" page is located at the end of the book and includes a brief bio about who the author is (or was). As publisher and editor of the novel, and as Leonard's nephew, I wanted to include a tad bit more; and my Aunt Louise (Leonard's wife) consented in letting me compose a foreword and an afterword.

Uncle Leonard was my favorite uncle, the cool uncle, the person who, as a kid, made you want to grow up and be *that* adult. I'm sure that my Aunt Louise or my cousins Jill & Danny (Leonard's children) might tell a different story — but I want you to see him as I did.

There was always something mysterious about my Uncle Leonard. He spent his career in the military, and when he finally retired he had achieved the rank of

Captain in the Air Force. During his time in the service, he was stationed all over the world from Turkey to Japan and would tell the most amazing stories of the places he had been and the people he had met. The characters he talked about always seemed like they had been torn out of an Ian Fleming novel. He adored James Bond and he passed that passion onto me as well. In fact, I remember on one visit we were watching a movie and James Bond dropped his famous Walther PPK. My uncle asked if I wanted to see one and proceeded to tour me through his impressive collection of guns and knives. My mother, as you can imagine, was none too happy.

You might envision some big tough military figure and not the gregarious little Jewish guy that would tell people that he simply was an economist for the military. My Aunt eschews this description but it is the one I recall my mother using. Of course, it was also my mother who would joke that my Uncle Leonard was really a spy.

A few years before he passed away, we were at a family gathering and he casually told us that the government had just declassified what he really did in the military. We all sat up to full attention for another round of stories. I can honestly say he was the real deal.

He had a passion for living. He built cars and boats, and spent the last 20+ years of his life as a retiree traveling with his wife throughout the United States, camping, RVing, and being with his family. Have you ever met someone while on vacation and told them "if you are ever up my way you should look me up?" Leonard was the guy that would actually look you up!

I only found out that he had written this novel after he passed away. But when I did, I was so excited to read it. Not just because I knew he had fulfilled his lifelong dream of writing a book but also because I would get to hear one more story from my favorite uncle. And unlike most stories he told — this one was meant for everyone to hear. This is my Uncle Leonard at his finest — telling his story on his terms.

The novel might be a work of fiction but there is an enormous amount of fact in it. He mined much of our family history and his own life experiences and put them into this book. Knowing this, I still wonder how much he made up and how much is true — but we will never know!

Leonard St. Clair Ross[1] passed away on July 10, 2009 and, ever the military man,

---

[1] How a Jewish boy from Cleveland came to have the middle name "St. Clair" is an entirely different story!

he was laid to rest at Arlington National Cemetery in Arlington, Virginia.

Leonard's wife Louise supervised the production of this book and hopes you enjoy *The Present Past* as much as we all do.

Jared Bendis

July 2017

PS I have one more note to share; but since it constitutes a spoiler, I placed it in the afterword — at the end of the book.

CHAPTER 1

The blanket of fog on the shore of the Bosporus was so thick that the twelve horses and their riders could not see one another even though they could hear the heavy breathing of the horse next to them as they raced along at breakneck speed towards their waiting ship. Baron Shafirov was beaming with pride. He had served his Tsar well. The eighteen months of his forced residence in Constantinople was a small price to pay for the army's safe return and the ending of hostilities with the Turks.

"Igor, not so fast," he yelled.

"Another hour or two in this barbaric place will not kill me, but these horses will if they lose their footing in this soup."

Igor Brodkin, captain in the Tsar's Imperial Guard had been sent to personally secure the safe return of the Baron Vice Chancellor and master negotiator of the treaty that had ended the war in 1711.

Even though the Baron had been given every comfort, including the comfort of some of the most beautiful women not selected for the Sultan's harem, he had been busy fulfilling a secret assignment given to him by the Tsar.

Several small velvet bags had been expertly sewn into the lining of his large pantaloons worn by the wealthy, well dressed of the court. It was a heavy load to be sure and he was anxious to discharge it to the treasure chest once he was safe on the waiting ship.

The sound of the horses' hooves suddenly changed to a hollow clickety-clack. The Baron knew that they must have reached the wharf area and his ship.

Igor cried out, "Prepare to set sail, Captain. I want to catch the tide before these barbarians change their minds and feed us to their dogs."

As the ship's sails filled and it silently slid through the water, the fog lifted slightly and Igor could see the palace of the Sultan. Now, there was a man who knew how to live, he thought. He was not like his Tsar, no gunpowder and smoke in his nostrils. While the Sultan wallowed in opulent splendor, his subjects barely had enough to eat at times. He realized that it was not much different in Russia. There would always be the few haves and the many have-nots.

The ship finally broke free of the fog as they entered the Marmara Sea. The huge warship, even though heavily laden with cannon, was one of the fastest in the fleet and could easily out sail the opposition. Tsar Peter the Great had chosen his shipbuilders well; Karsten Brant was one of the finest and had done himself proud when he built the "Catherine".

The Captain knocked on the cabin door. The Baron quickly turned the large key in the chest, placed it in his coat and said, "Come". The Captain stepped into the cabin.

"Where to now, your Excellency? I am at your complete disposal."

The Baron smiled. It had been awhile since he had been called "your Excellency".

"I must confer with Igor before I can decide. I still have that wretched smell of fish in my nostrils. We had a long ride along the Bosporus and it seemed as if the fish were swimming in the fog itself. What is our strength on board?" asked the Baron.

The captain paused, then said,

"We have 150 of the most loyal guardsmen. My crew is handpicked by me personally and my gunners can place a ball in the blowhole of a whale on the second shot, to be sure.

"How are our provisions?" asked the Baron.

"Six months, no problem. After that, we will be eating like most Russians".

Just then, Igor knocked on the cabin door,

"Come" said the Baron.

Igor ducked as he came through the doorway. He was almost as tall as the Tsar himself. At six feet six inches he was a formidable looking soldier.

"We must talk," he said.

"Captain, would you excuse us! Just stay on this heading until we are through the Dardanelle's and into the Aegean. Your devotion and loyalty to the Tsar will be noted in my dispatch, which I will send at our first landfall."

The captain saluted and left the cabin.

"Sit, Igor my rescuer. I cannot thank you enough for our safe exit from the clutches of the Sultan. I knew I would come to no harm, but eighteen months is a long time and I wondered whether the Turks would ever be satisfied that the Tsar had kept his bargain. You know what I have in my possession?"

"The Tsar himself briefed me," Igor said.

"Does anyone else know, Igor?"

"No one, your Excellency"

"Good. Even the most loyal could be swayed by just one of my pretties. The Tsar has paid dearly for our cargo and we must deliver it to him in all haste."

The Baron leaned back in his chair and yawned.

"It will be a long trip home, Igor. How long do you think?"

Igor thought a moment.

"How long a stop at our first landfall?"

"Just long enough to dispatch a message to the Tsar and pick up one passenger," said the Baron.

"It is 2,500 leagues to St. Petersburg, at least. If we have good weather and fair winds, we should be home in three months."

"You are not only a good soldier, but a knowledgeable navigator, too," smiled the Baron.

"I get a little seasick, but there is no safer way to safeguard our cargo."

The Baron rose from his chair and gave Igor a big bear hug.

"Inform the Captain and tell him to set a course for Marseille. Let us show our transom to any and all ships. We are not to fire unless fired upon. Make yourself and your men comfortable, Captain Igor Brodkin. I am recommending your promotion to, at least, Colonel, and with your continued good performance, you will be a General in no time," mused Baron Shafirov.

CHAPTER 2

The wind drove the "Catherine" at such a speed, that the dolphins that had joined her in the Aegean thought she was a fellow traveler. As they rounded Cape Teulada at the tip of Sardinia, the Baron called a meeting with the Captain of the Ship and Igor.

"We should be in Marseille in at least three days at the pace we have been going" he said.

"We have been very fortunate," responded the Captain.

"It is a good omen," chimed in Igor.

"Our stop will be a short one. For all outward appearances, we are on a diplomatic mission from the Tsar. That is all the local bureaucrats need to know."

"Can I give my crew time ashore, your Excellency?" asked the Captain.

"To be sure, one night, each man to have a brother, so they can keep out of trouble and return safely."

"What about my Guards," asked Igor?

"I am sorry, Igor, they must stay on board; half of the men on duty at all times. But I will tell you what. A party is in order. Recruit some local beauties, bring them aboard, everything above board, you know what I mean. Buy some extra fine provisions from the local merchants and convey to the men the compliments of their Tsar for a fine job thus far and the expected completion of the mission, because our next stop is St. Petersburg." ordered the Baron.

"Now, Captain, if you will excuse me, I would speak to Igor in private."

"As you wish, your Excellency," replied the Captain, as he saluted and left the cabin.

"Igor, now down to serious business," said the Baron.

"When we dock you will direct one of your most trusted men to hire a carriage and proceed to Avignon. Once there, he will go to the house of Monsieur Le Grange on Rue de la Coq. He is expecting a messenger from me. There will be a required password. Listen well," smiled the Baron.

"It is 'Little Mother. Monsieur Le Grange will return with your man to the ship'," said the Baron.

"He is an older gentleman, so make every effort to make him comfortable on the return trip. He is the finest in his craft and the Tsar is expecting him to do great things for him," said the Baron.

"Secondly, you will send a courier to the Tsar. I will give you a dispatch, and with good weather, he should reach our friends in Hamburg in four days and then, a fast passage to St. Petersburg. I am anxious to let the Tsar know of our progress. I have not sent a communiqué to him since we left Constantinople," said the Baron.

"Everything will be as you have ordered," replied Igor.

"Let us have a drink on that, my friend," said the Baron.

He rose from his chair and went to the locker, removing a bottle of brandy and two small glasses. He poured the rich looking liquid into each and handed one to Igor.

"To the Tsar, Peter the Great," toasted the Baron.

"And to Catherine, the Little Mother," seconded Igor.

The following two days passed quickly. The crew had a grand time on their liberty ashore. The innkeepers loved their money and the local girls loved them. Avignon was not far and the roads were dry. The carriage with its four horses made an easy trip of it and Monsieur Le Grange arrived at the ship only slightly ruffled by the rough roads. He was welcomed warmly by the Baron, and shown to his cabin. Within the hour, the lines were cast ashore and, once again, the "Catherine" unfurled her sails and headed South-by-South west, towards the Straits of Gibraltar and home.

CHAPTER 3

They had been at sea three weeks since Marseille and were already entering the Baltic Sea. The summer sun warmed them and the winds cooled them as they sped along their appointed way.

The Baron and Monsieur Le Grange sat on deck and spoke in quiet whispers.

"In all my years, your Excellency, I have never seen such magnificence," said the old gentleman.

"How you obtained them is an unbelievable stroke of genius."

"Constantinople is a Mecca for the merchants of the world. It seems that everyone wants to buy the favor of the Sultan. Some do, some do not. I was at the right place at the right time. Once I found out who were the suppliers at the source, I was able to negotiate some trading for them. I cannot go into detail as to what, but I can assure you the cost was great. The war with Sweden has strained the treasury of the Tsar, so I had to barter for our cargo with whatever the Tsar would let me have." The Baron stopped speaking as the Captain approached them.

"St. Petersburg by the end of the week, gentlemen," he said.

"Well done, Captain," replied the Baron. "Your loyalty and devotion to duty has been already made known to the Tsar. I would expect that he already has plans for you in his growing fleet. If your gunners can shoot as well as you sail, I pity the Swedes."

True to his words, the "Catherine", quietly and without fanfare, was moored in the harbor at St. Petersburg by weeks end. The Baron made his goodbyes to the Captain of the ship. He thanked the crew who cheered him as he stepped ashore.

Igor saluted the Baron smartly and said," I know I will see you again, thank you for your kind words and, if ever you need someone to go sailing with, you know whom to call."

The Baron laughed at that. Igor had a fine wit to boot.

After a heavy chest had been loaded into the waiting carriage, the Baron and Monsieur Le Grange were whisked away to the Summer Palace on the Neva; two dozen guardsmen and their mounts bringing up the rear.

St. Petersburg had grown substantially in the last few years. Not only had many new stone buildings and beautiful homes been built, ships from many different countries were using the new port facilities. Many government offices that the Baron remembered seeing in Moscow were now located in St. Petersburg. To be sure, there were still many ramshackle wooden structures here and there, but, overall, a new city was taking form and the Tsar was making it happen as fast as he could.

An Italian, Domenico Trezzini, designed the Summer Palace. The Tsar had encouraged such qualified men as he, to come to St. Petersburg and help in the development of his great dream.

"Well, Monsieur Le Grange! What do you think of our new capitol to be?"

"I am very impressed. It is not Paris, to be sure, but I can see a real majestic beauty developing within this place. I am honored that the Tsar has chosen me to contribute in some small way," answered Monsieur Le Grange.

"When will I meet the Tsar?" asked the Frenchman.

"First, we will take you to a lovely house with a workshop that has been provided for you. Driver! You there! What is our first stop?"

The Driver opened a small slide in the roof of the carriage and briefly looked down upon his passengers.

"Your Excellency, my instructions are to take your guest to a new house not far from the Summer Palace. It is a lovely spot with a view of the river."

"After you are settled in and have found your way around, I will arrange a quiet reception with the Tsar." said the Baron. "Today, I must bring the Tsar up to date on my sojourn in Constantinople. He knows that I know how to strike a bargain, but for some reason, he thinks I can read the minds of the Turks", mused the Baron.

Just then, the carriage drew to a stop and the guardsmen riding shotgun jumped down and motioned to the officer leading the troop following the carriage. The officer dismounted, rubbed the neck of his horse and walked over to the carriage.

"Gentlemen, we have arrived. My men will assist you with your bags and, for your safety, two of them will post themselves around the house," said the officer.

"For my safety!" exclaimed Monsieur Le Grange.

"Be careful, Monsieur, no one must know our business," the Baron whispered quietly in his ear.

"My pardon, Baron, I am but a humble craftsman and not familiar with stealth and secrets," said the old gentleman.

The baggage was carried into the house. The Baron said goodbye and Monsieur Le Grange settled down in a comfortable chair. A servant stepped forward and asked him, "Are you hungry, Sir? We have some excellent duck, prepared by the chef to the Tsar this morning, especially for you."

"I do believe I will," he replied.

The food was served. Monsieur Le Grange ate to contentment and once finished, yawned, rubbed his eyes and sought out his bedroom where he stretched out on a very comfortable bed, to his surprise.

CHAPTER 4

Once his guest had been dispatched, the Baron and his cargo proceeded to the Summer Palace. The carriage drew up in front of the long entrance steps and six imperial guardsmen escorted the Baron and his chest into a small drawing room. He had not been there but a moment when he heard a loud voice in the doorway.

"You have finally arrived! Welcome, my dear Baron Vice Chancellor. I cannot tell you how sorely you have been missed in your absence. Your dispatch from France was most appreciated and now, before you make your report and show me what you have brought, I want to bring you up to date on our military victories."

The speaker was no less than six feet eight inches tall. His muscular frame could have qualified him to wrestle a bear. He was the Tsar of all the Russians, Peter the Great, in every respect.

Baron Shafirov bowed and said," Your imperial majesty, the forced vacation in Constantinople was worth every minute to guarantee your safety and that of your army."

"Well said," replied the Tsar. "Sit down my friend, you must be tired after your long trip."

The Tsar was in an excellent mood. He recounted how his armies had penetrated into Finland and how he was developing his naval fleet to engage the enemy in the Baltic. He was the consummate general.

"Now that I have told you all that I have been doing," chimed the Tsar. "Show me what you have brought for me."

The Baron slid the heavy chest from under the table. He removed a large key from his coat and he opened the chest. The sunlight coming in the window was immediately captured by the contents of the chest. The brilliant reflection of light was almost blinding.

The Tsar gasped in amazement. "You told me what you had been able to get, but

I had no idea that their beauty and size were so magnificent."

The Baron scooped up a handful and spread them on the table. The diamonds were as large as walnuts. Their brilliance and color was unlike anything the Tsar had ever seen. The Baron reached down again into another compartment of the chest. Up came rubies, a red as beautiful as the setting sun. Once more, he reached down into the magical box and withdrew sapphires, the color of the clear summer sky and emeralds of a green never before seen.

"I know you will have more than enough stones to have Monsieur Le Grange fashion for you a necklace of unsurpassed beauty. It is truly a magnificent present for an Empress," said the Baron.

"I shall give it to her on her coronation," exclaimed the Tsar.

CHAPTER 5

The Pan Am 707 jet braked to a stop not far from the entrance to the airport at Yesilkoy. Among the passengers departing first was a tall man about six feet, wiry and yet, very muscular.

"Josh, over here," a voice cried out. "Good to see you again."

Gabe Smith, Consul at the American Consulate in Istanbul, extended his hand in a warm greeting to Josh Ross; a fellow diplomat recently arrived from Washington.

"How long has it been? 8 or 9 years? The last time I saw you was in Israel and the Israelis were hell bent for the Suez Canal and we had no idea how we were going to solve that problem if they did not give it back."

Josh looked at Gabe and gave him a quiet smile. His friend, who was really more than a friend, had also been a guiding force in his early days in the diplomatic corps back in 1956.

"You look great," said Josh. "I hope I look as good as you do when retirement is right around the corner!"

"I have been following your career, young fellow. You are quite the troubleshooter these days. I hope you do not get too close to the tanks on the border. These Turks have a hair trigger and would just love to have a fight with their Greek neighbors."

Once again, hostilities had broken out between Turkey and Greece and Josh had been sent to see what he could do to slow the juices flowing through the veins of the combatants. He had matured a lot since the Suez War. His ability to bring out the best in the people he negotiated with was highly recognized among those who plied his craft. Being a Jew did not always help. But his knowledge of the ancient laws, his gift of wit and philosophical intuition, put a smile on people's faces and put them at ease. He was being called upon more and more to meet with some of the more difficult personalities who seemed to spring up overnight in various far flung places of the world.

"What's first on your agenda, Josh? Are you going on to Ankara?"

"The action is not far from here, I understand," said Josh. "Most of the higher ups involved will be meeting here in town. I don't think this is a real big deal. Some askers got drunk, made a ruckus at the border, and the Greeks called out the National Guard. I think that once they understand the nature of the invasion and see the alcohol level of the invaders, they will back up their tanks and return to base."

"You always make it sound so simple", said Gabe. "Anything you need, anything, just let me know. I have access to resources you would not believe. Oh! Before I forget, I have a small packet for you that was sent to your home in Monterey. You not being there, your neighbor thought it was important, so he sent it to the State Department and they whisked it to me here."

"I am tired, Gabe. I have a reservation over at the Hilton. I need some rest before I meet with whomever. So, if I can get a lift to the hotel, I would be much obliged."

"I want to have a chance to talk with you, perhaps over dinner," said Gabe. "It has been a long time."

"That is a great idea. I hear they have some great restaurants along the Bosporus. I am a real jerk though, how is Mary? Still as beautiful as ever?"

"You had better believe it," said Gabe. "How about seven thirty?"

Josh looked at his Rolex GMT. It was two o'clock local time. He would have time to read his mail, take a shower and a short nap.

"Seven thirty it is then," said Josh.

Gabe left to meet with some customs officials at the airport and had offered his car and driver to Josh. The Turkish driver was very good. He could weave in and out of traffic, like they drive at Sebring. With no traffic lights, this was no mean feat. As the four-lane highway ended and they approached the gates to the city, Josh was amazed at the condition of the huge wall surrounding the area.

"I bet this goes back a ways," he said.

The driver smiled and said," Everything in Istanbul is very old and some of our oldest buildings and mosques are in the best condition."

The city was crowded with traffic and people in every form of dress. The Hilton was located in a better part of the city proper and the people going in and out were dressed a lot like Josh, casual, but elegant. He thanked the driver and entered the hotel. He handed his small suitcase to the bellhop and, after checking in, was shown to his room where he plopped down on the bed, closed his eyes and thanked the good Lord, once again, for a safe journey half way around the world.

As Josh slept, other events were taking place, which would have a long lasting effect on his activities. Not far from the area of the hotel an elite group of individuals were discussing Josh's recent arrival in the city. The Bulgarian consulate was, among other things, a hotbed of spying activity for the Russians. They followed everything and anything having to do with any Westerner coming to their area.

Colonel Sloven, chief investigator for the Bulgarians in that area, was keenly interested in Josh's arrival. He knew all about the tiff between the Greeks and the Turks. He believed that there were other reasons that brought Josh to Istanbul. He wanted Josh's every move watched. He wanted to know the names of every individual Josh met. He was certain there was more to his visit than met the eye. He ordered a dossier on Josh from his counterpart in the KGB.

"You are making too much of this," said his confederate Christos. "The American is a low level bureaucrat. He has nothing to do with what we are interested in."

"So, you are now the expert and know everything that I am interested in. Perhaps I should go on vacation to the Black Sea since you are now so smart. Get me that dossier yesterday, no excuses," said Sloven. And with that the meeting ended.

Josh felt refreshed. Nothing like a short nap in the middle of the day to take the edge off what had to be done. He reached over and opened his briefcase. He had almost forgotten about the packet that Gabe had given him. His knife easily cut through the thick tape banding the packet. It was most interesting that the letter was not addressed to him. It had been sent to his father, who had been dead for many years. The letter was two years old. Whoever sent it did not know that his father was not alive.

The letter had bounced around quite a bit until it reached him through the magic of the Postal Service, and their system of forwarding mail until it finds a final resting place. He was indebted to his neighbor for sending it on to the State Department.

He sliced open the envelope and took out two handwritten pages. Just his luck, they were written in Russian and came from Moscow. The letter was dated September 15, 1963.

"Now what am I going to do!" he exclaimed out loud. Just then the telephone rang. He picked it up. "Yes".

"Josh, is that you? You sound funny." It was Gabe. "I will send my driver for you, the fellow who drove you from the airport," said Gabe. "He should be there about seven-fifteen. Meet him in front of the hotel. Mary and I will meet you at the restaurant, if you don't mind."

"No problem," said Josh. "See you soon."

CHAPTER 6

As they sped along the road on the Bosporus, the lights from the cafes dazzled the eyes. There were many people out for a walk in the cool night air. The smell of fish was very strong. The driver braked to a stop in front of one of the brightest lit restaurants just as a black Citroen sped by, swerving to miss a car parked with its rear end sticking out too much, and sliding into an empty spot about five cars up the street.

"Thanks again for the ride, effendim," he said.

"I will return in several hours after your dinner," replied the driver.

As Josh exited the car, he patted the letter in his pocket. He wanted to be sure he had not forgotten it.

Mary and Gabe were seated at a small table in the rear. The restaurant was filled with delightful smells and the music of rich violins.

"Hi, there," said Josh. "Beautiful place; do you come here often?"

"Hi, yourself," said Mary. "Long time no see."

"This is our favorite place," replied Gabe.

Drinks were ordered all around and the dinner followed shortly thereafter. Each night, a different entrée was served and there was only one. Tonight it was lamb.

"The years have been kind to you, Josh," said Mary. "You both look great, too. You're just as I remember you since we were together in Tel Aviv."

Josh broke off his conversation and turned abruptly to Gabe.

"Do you read Russian?" he said.

"Not well enough to do any good. Why do you ask?"

Josh withdrew the letter from his jacket, and handed it to Gabe.

"This is what was in the packet you gave me this afternoon. It's handwritten in Russian. It's postmarked Moscow and was written almost three years ago. I have no idea what it is about or who it is from." Josh paused for a few moments. "I hesitate to have it translated by anyone in the Department. It could be from a close relative and then there goes my security clearance before I even have a chance to defend myself. Confidentially, old buddy, one friend to another, what do you think I should do?"

Gabe stared at Josh and then at the letter. This could be damaging, he thought.

"Isn't André originally from Russia?" said Mary

"André Zommer, Yes, very good, Mary. Good idea. I have heard him speak Russian often to some of his students at the college. He must be able to read it also. He has no connection to anything we do and, being a friend, I am sure he will be very discreet and keep everything confidential. I will call him first thing tomorrow and arrange a meeting for you," said Gabe.

CHAPTER 7

André Zommer, physical education director at Robert's College, was a long time resident of Istanbul. He was a study all by himself and the experiences of his lifetime could have filled the pages of a best seller. He was not surprised to hear from Gabe Smith. Many times, he had been called by the First Consul to handle delicate matters for the Americans. Looking out at the Bosporus through his office window, he wondered what the young man Gabe was sending him would need in the line of help. It always happened that way. A simple letter to translate was never simple. Nothing ever was. The last time he had been involved with Americans, he had gone all the way to Pakistan on a very simple job to negotiate the release of an American military person, who according to official records, never even existed. Ah!

Anything to break up the boredom, even at his age.

The knock on the door brought him out of his daydreaming.

"Come," he said.

The door opened and Josh entered a room, which had all the attributes of one of the finest antique stores in Paris. The man sitting behind the huge, walnut desk was the spitting image of the benefactor of "Little Orphan Annie", Daddy Warbucks.

André Zommer stepped from behind his desk and gave a warm greeting to his visitor.

"Welcome to Istanbul, Mr. Ross. I trust you are enjoying the sights of one of the oldest cities in this part of the world."

"Not as yet," replied Josh. "I just arrived yesterday and, be as it may, I have been distracted from my work by the arrival of a letter mailed from Moscow a long time ago and written in Russian. I have to know its contents as it may have a direct bearing on my work."

André moved back to the window and gazed out at the Bosporus. The light reflected off his shiny bald head. His white suit was a tailor's work of art and it fit his six foot four frame perfectly. He was a powerful looking man; about sixty years old, Josh guessed.

"Let's see that letter of yours, but, first, how about some Turkish coffee? It has the ability to perk up your senses with uncanny swiftness."

Josh agreed, and André made a call on his intercom. Several minutes later, a knock on the door ushered in a lovely brunette carrying a tray of coffee and the most delicate cups Josh had ever seen. The young woman spoke to André in an unusual accent. Josh was sure she wasn't Turkish and thought she might be Israeli.

"This is Sarah, my assistant," said André.

Josh smiled at her and said," A pleasure to meet you."

He looked closely at the striking beauty of this woman. Her skin was satin smooth and had a natural suntan. Her features were delicate and her figure was very athletic.

"Thank you, Sarah. I will call you if I need you for anything."

"I hope you have a pleasant visit," she said as she left the room.

André handed Josh the coffee and they both sat down to savor their drinks. Josh pulled the letter from his jacket pocket, handing it to André. André read the letter and said,

"The letter is addressed to Abraham Rosofsky. Who is Abraham Rosofsky?" asked André.

"That was my father, our family name was Americanized to Ross when he immigrated." replied Josh.

"The letter is from a cousin living in Moscow. It says that a sister of your father, who was left behind in Russia many years ago, is no longer alive.

"The cousin wishes you well and, if at all possible, asks for your help to send medicine, the latest antibiotics if possible.

"The letter speaks of Yeshica Rosofsky. The letter writer speaks of him with great reverence and devotion and tells your father that he loved his 'uncle' Yeshica very much.

"Who is Yeshica Rosofsky?"

"He was my grandfather, but I never knew very much about him. He died a long time ago," said Josh.

"Mr. Ross," André said in an unusual tone.

"I want to continue this discussion with you, but not here in my office." He pointed to the walls, then to his ears. Josh got the message.

They both rose and walked to the door. Once outside, in the cool spring air, André directed Josh to a bench on the lawn overlooking the Bosporus.

"Sit, my young friend. I have much to discuss with you. First off, where was your Father born?"

"I remember his naturalization documents listed a village outside of Kiev," said Josh.

"What did your father do in Russia for a living?"

"He was just a young boy in his years in Russia. He lived on a big, ranch type farm where he said, my grandfather raised horses. My father left Russia in 1916 and came to America with his mother when he was seventeen. One more thing, my father said that my grandfather was an officer in the army."

André gave Josh a long, slow stare. Josh could feel the intensity of Andrés gaze as his eyes bore into him. André spoke very softly. There was a glint of sweat on his face and Josh could see a tremble in his hands.

"I knew your grandfather. He was a very great man."

Josh felt a flush all over his body. But, then he collected himself and replied with a bit of laughter.

"My grandfather died in 1905 in the Russo-Japanese war. This is 1965 and you look to be about sixty years old. How could you have possibly known him?!"

"Thank you for your nice compliment. I am ninety," André replied. "I served under your grandfather for many years as a staff officer. He was a field marshal in the Tsar's army and he was one of their best."

It was then that Josh felt the lightning bolt, although there was not a cloud in the sky and the sun shone brightly overhead.

"This is unbelievable," Josh stammered. "You must tell me everything you know about him."

"First things first," André said. "I never know when my office is bugged. I did not want anyone to know what I just told you about myself and, least of all, what I have just told you about your grandfather. Yes, your grandfather was killed. I was in the same battle when it happened. A shell landed not far from him. Although your grandfather was one of the best horsemen in all of Russia, when his horse bolted from the concussion, it fell on him and he died instantly. A very sad day for us all."

Again, Josh stared at André, his mouth slightly agape in wonderment at what he was just told.

"Tsar Alexander II had great admiration and respect for your grandfather. As a teenager living near Kiev, he became famous for his feats of horsemanship and his ability to manage horses. Alexander chose your grandfather to come to Moscow and teach his young sons, Nicholas and Alexander, to ride .As a reward for his devotion to his sons, Alexander sent your grandfather to the military academy to become an officer in the army. The Tsar then rewarded your grandfather financially by giving him a huge horse ranch as a life estate, to raise horses to sell to the army. Your grandfather had a friend whom he made his partner in the ranch, and it was he who ran the ranch while your grandfather fought the Tsar's battles. But that is only half of it. Your grandfather was a favorite of the Tsarina herself. It was she, rumor says, who engineered the gift of the horse ranch and the life estate."

"I do not know what to say," Josh exclaimed. "This is all so unbelievable."

While Josh and André continued to converse, not far away, two men in a black Citroen sat watching their every move.

"What do you think our baldheaded friend is telling the American?" asked the one called Novikov.

"I wish that we had the new listening equipment the KGB promised us," said his cohort, Feodor.

"We are going to have to make a full report to Dzerzhinsky about this meeting, and I do not have anything specific to tell him about the conversation," said Novikov. "Let's make something up. I have a promotion coming up and I need the extra pay. My new apartment in Ulus costs 3,000 lira a month and I am not going to give it up just because I could not tell that crazy KGB officer in Moscow every word the American spoke while here in Istanbul."

"I will have to think about that," said Feodor. And with that, he started the car and drove off at a high rate of speed.

André noticed the black Citroen and motioned to Josh to look in its direction.

"I think those are our friends from the Russian consulate. If it were the Bulgarians they would have been more discreet and we would have never noticed them," said André.

"I want to continue our talk, Josh. I want to tell you all I can remember about your grandfather and how I met him, and of the battle of Mukden where he was killed. There is also one other matter, which has troubled me these many years, that I think you should be aware of. We must meet where we cannot be overheard. For some reason, the Bulgarians and the Russians have been very active in the last few days. I hope that it is not because of you."

"I need a few days to do what I came here for," Josh said. "I am glad that I have cleared up the letter from Moscow. If it had been a close relative, I would have had to report it to my superiors and I am afraid that would have put a damper on my activities, to say the least."

"The letter writer, your cousin, knew your grandfather," said André. "He is, or was, older than I am, if he is alive at all. The letter was written about two years ago.

"I will have Sarah call you in a couple of days and set a time and place for us to meet. Until then, be careful and good luck," André said.

CHAPTER 8

Josh was not far off in his analysis of the border dispute. It had been some irate asker who had gotten drunk and driven a tank over the border. His fellow comrades followed him to bring him back, but before they realized their position, they were over a kilometer into Greece. The Turks have a special way of handling problems of this nature. Punishment is swift and not always just.

The bureaucrats and the diplomats on both sides realized that tanks on each side of the border staring each other down was not the best way for allies in NATO to cooperate with one another. The dispute was settled, until the next time, and Josh was certain that there would be a next time.

Istanbul was a beautiful city. The Bosporus flowed between the old and the new cities. The shores were lined with old forts, palaces, and apartment houses high up on the hills. Russian ships plied their way South. Warships were seen from time to time and even a submarine would surface, which by international law, was mandatory when passing through the straits. Ferries darted back and forth, carrying cars and people. Along the shores, rows of trucks lined up for their turn to cross, usually at night when other traffic was down. Now and then, a modern-looking sailboat could be seen and even a racing scull, appearing to be going nowhere in particular.

Josh thought about the conversation he had with André the other day, as he lay on his bed at the Hilton. He also thought about Sarah, André's assistant. He had not noticed a wedding ring on her finger. Perhaps this would be an opportunity to get to know her better. He wondered what the other matter was that André had alluded to. How could his grandfather ever have made it so high in the ranks of the Tsar's army? He was a Jew. Alexander II treated the Jews better than the other Tsars. But Alexander III was an anti-Semite if there ever was one, as well as his son, Nicholas. The pogroms during his reign were infamous. And yet, André had said that Nicholas and my grandfather were friends from boyhood. How did my grandfather become a general and then to be a field marshal? Well, these were all unanswered questions that he hoped André would answer. The telephone's ring brought him out of his deep thoughts.

"Hello"

"Mr. Ross, this is Sarah.

"Yes, Sarah, how nice to hear your voice again. Please call me Josh."

"I know that you are not that familiar with the city; is that correct?" she said.

"Absolutely. What do you suggest?"

"André thought it best that I pick you up at the hotel and we go together to meet him," she said.

"I agree. What time?"

"How about two o'clock?"

"That's fine. See you in front of the Hilton at two," replied Josh.

"Goodbye, Josh."

The phone was quiet for a minute and then rang again.

"Yes," said Josh.

"Hi, Josh. It's Gabe. I heard about your meeting with the combatants. As always, you hit the nail on the head. Pride runs deep on both sides and no one likes to give an inch. There is an intense hatred there and it goes back a long way. I would not be surprised if someday the Turks run every single Greek out of Turkey. As a new face with a reputation for fairness, they both accepted your proposals and, hopefully, we will be incident free for the remainder of the year. How did your meeting with André go?"

"I meant to call you earlier," said Josh. "There was so much to tell you and I did not want to go into detail on the phone.

"I got you there, Buddy," said Gabe.

"I am meeting with André today. After I see him, we should meet and I'll fill you in on the whole story."

"Just give me a call when you are ready. See you soon." And Gabe hung up.

As Josh started to get ready for his meeting, the air outside his hotel window was pierced by the high wail of a voice on a megaphone, which could not be misunderstood. It was the call to prayer and all devout Moslems throughout the city heeded its call.

At a meeting not far away from Josh's hotel, in the basement of the Bulgarian consulate, Colonel Sloven and Christos were deep in discussion.

"I am tired of that meddling old fool getting in our way," said Christos.

"The American met with him two days ago and now our contact at the hotel says that he plans to meet with him again today, but, as yet, I do not know where."

"Maybe it is time to put him out of his misery," replied Sloven.

"I can make it look like an accident, Colonel. No one will know the difference. Since he is just an old teacher who has lived well past his usefulness, no one will suspect foul play."

"Christos, you forget that the Russians are also watching the American. We know why he came here, but we do not know why he is meeting with the teacher. I spoke to Dzerzhinsky this morning. He, too, thinks there are too many players in the game here. He has some clout, this fellow. You know that he is the grandson of Felix Dzerzhinsky, one of the first directors of the Cheka, the forerunner of the KGB."

"So what does he want us to do and why does he have such a special interest in the American?" said Christos.

"That he did not confide in me," replied Sloven."But Dzerzhinsky thought it would be a good idea if we scared the old man a bit. Maybe he will stop meddling in politics and stick to teaching."

"Do we need to contact Novikov at the Russian consulate?" said Christos.

"We have our instructions and they have theirs. I am not a Russian citizen yet, and I am not planning to become one soon," said Sloven. "Scare the old teacher. Make it look like an accident. Do not let anyone see you. And do it today. Do not kill him. Break a few bones."

The taxi pulled up in front of the Hilton just as Josh stepped out of the front door. Sarah waved, opened the door, and Josh slid in beside her.

"Where are we going?" he said.

"Rumeli Hisari, lutfen," Sarah said to the driver. "That is the old fort on the European side of the Bosporus, to the North of the city. Five hundred years ago, when the Ottomans invaded, they blockaded the city by stretching a chain across the Bosporus to another fort on the

Asian side. The fort was built in ninety days by thousands of workers. It is still in excellent repair. André thought we would look like tourists discussing the history," said Sarah.

"Fine by me," Josh replied.

The traffic was not bad and the driver sped quickly and expertly through side streets until he reached the road along the Bosporus. It was not long before the huge stone structure came into view. High up in the ramparts, a tall man in a white suit could be seen, the sun reflecting off his bald head. Josh and Sarah exited the cab and climbed the stone stairs. Josh greeted André and the three of them sat down on the low stone wall to talk.

"Do you mind if Sarah listens to my story, Josh?" said André. "I have been wanting to fill her in on this ever since I found out that you were the grandson of Marshal Rosofsky. She is privy to many of my secrets; I trust her as my own daughter and I do not want to exclude her."

"You are the storyteller," said Josh. "There are a few questions I would like to ask you. You can answer them as you tell me the story. The first one is; did you know that my grandfather was a Jew? Secondly, how did he become a general? Third, how and when did he become a field marshal? And lastly, you mentioned that something had been troubling you for a long time, which I thought, had something to do with my grandfather's death."

"I will address each of these in my story," said André. "It was a long time ago. I was sixteen years old. I always wanted to be an officer in the military. My family had a long history of military service. My mother had a distant relative who had been a general for Peter the Great. Their family name had been Brodkin. When I was in the military academy, the exploits of your grandfather were already legend. As a young officer in the Russo-Turkish war in 1877, he showed himself to be courageous, daring, intelligent, and a superb strategist. The war went slowly for Russia. Many of the soldiers did not even have the right cartridges for their rifles.

"It was at the siege of Plevna that your grandfather, then Major Rosofsky, led the charge that breached the walls. He then went on with the cavalry to raid and seize many Balkan forts and towns. Finally, only a month or so later, the army had advanced on Adrianople and taken it. Once again, it was your grandfather who was in the thick of it, rallying the men to attack. For this, he was promoted to Colonel."

André got up and stretched, walked around for a bit, then sat back down on the wall.

"Many of the problems of this war were studied by Colonel Rosofsky and the general staff. He made many recommendations to his superiors, which were followed through, making the army stronger. To my knowledge, during this whole time, no one knew that your grandfather was a Jew. His ranch prospered. His reputation grew and his career was on a solid footing. It was only a matter of time before he would be promoted to general.

"Shortly before his assassination, Alexander II rewarded your grandfather for all his past service and loyalty. He promoted him to general. When I became an officer, Alexander III lay dying in his bed. My first assignment was as an aide to General Rosofsky. I did not know that he was a Jew, and if I had known, it would not have mattered. I remember the first time I met him. He was almost six feet tall and every inch a general.

"The men loved him and would have followed him to Hell and back. Character is something that is always visible no matter how one chooses to wear it. Your grandfather had character and conviction.

Nicholas II called on General Rosofsky for advice on many occasions. Nicholas had revered his father and his grandfather, Alexander II, and knew of their respect for your grandfather.

"But let us focus on his character. Your grandfather was ordered to conduct a pogrom on a Jewish town not far from Kiev. Now that I know your grandfather was a Jew, I understand fully his reasons for doing what he did. His army advanced on the small town. A river filled with breaking ice lay between him and the town. His orders were specific. It was before Easter. Kill all the Jews that were there. General Rosofsky stood on the edge of the river and surveyed what was before him. I remember his exact words as if it were yesterday.

"I will not sacrifice one solitary soldier for those filthy Jews," he said.

"He turned his army back from the ice filled river and no one crossed into the town. The people were spared. This is character. He could have been court-martialed for that act."

Josh rose from the wall. He was thrilled at what he had just heard. He had goose bumps all over him. They all needed a break. Josh spotted a man selling tea not far away.

"Would you like some tea, Sarah," he said?

"I would love some," Sarah replied.

"One more, with no sugar." said André.

The tea was served and they all sat down again. André gazed out upon the Bosporus, as a Russian freighter glided south toward the Marmora Sea.

CHAPTER 9

The black Citroen was once again parked ominously on the road along the shore. Christos, the lone driver, sat appearing to read a newspaper and he was not enjoying the long period of waiting. He wanted to get the dirty job over with as soon as possible.

André started to speak again. "Nicholas II's coronation in 1894 was magnificent. General Rosofsky and his staff were invited. Your grandmother was there also. She looked like a queen herself. She was a very beautiful woman. The Empress Aleksandra was there wearing a magnificent gown and, around her neck, was a necklace of diamonds, rubies, sapphires and emeralds, so brilliant and dazzling, that they alone could have lit up the Kremlin palace. The necklace was none other than that which had been given by

Peter the Great to his Empress Catherine. There was none like it anywhere. It was priceless. Nicholas called your grandfather over to his side and laughed with him about something. I felt proud to be serving a man who could laugh with the Tsar. But then, I was young and what did I know.

"Your grandfather made many trips to his ranch outside of Kiev. I went with him on several occasions. It was a very large ranch and there were thousands of horses grazing on the land. I remember seeing a little toddler of a boy. He was probably your father. The horses were transferred to the army's cavalry training unit. Your grandfather had done a fine job. These were some of the best mounts in Russia.

"The Trans-Siberian railroad had been started and thousands of troops were being moved into the Far-Eastern areas. Japan grew bolder and stronger. Japan and Russia had many differences and they were not being resolved.

"The Japanese attacked our fleet at Port Arthur. It was disastrous for Russia. Your grandfather was called to the Winter Palace in St. Petersburg. The strikes had begun and thousands were protesting living conditions and wages. The workers blockaded the streets. The soldiers were ordered to fire upon the crowds. Hundreds were killed; it was truly a bloody Sunday. The reprisal was swift. The Governor–General of Moscow was blown to bits by a revolutionary. The Tsar and the Tsarina were very disturbed by the turn of events. They did not know who might be next on the list of assassinations by the revolutionary groups. Your grandfather advised them not to go out in public anymore. Not to attend the funeral of the Governor-General and to seclude themselves in the Alexander palace at Tsarskoye Selo.

"The Tsar Nicholas II promoted your grandfather to Field Marshal. He directed him to use any and all resources to fend off the Japanese in a land attack, which he knew was coming soon. He said he would send his best fleet to battle the Japanese and hope for the best. He wanted him to leave immediately as it was over 8000 kilometers by rail to the battle area.

"Now this next bit of information is what has troubled me these past sixty years, I was not there to see it. I speak only of rumor. I have no proof of what I am going to tell you. The Tsarina, fearing for her life and that of her husband and children, called your grandfather aside and entrusted to him something of great value, which she thought he could safeguard better than anyone. And if the worst came, he would be able to use this treasure to help save the Russian people. Her remorse over the deaths of so many people in recent days and the threat on the lives of her family had driven her to desperate measures."

CHAPTER 10

Marshal Rosofsky called André aside. "Gather the staff and let us proceed at once to the troop depot at St. Petersburg. We do not have a moment to lose. We are proceeding at once to Harbin. The Japanese will pay dearly for their sneak attack on our fleet. One Russian soldier is worth four Japanese and we will drive them back into the sea from where they came."

The shrill whistle of the steam, blasting from the two locomotives loaded with troops, pierced the night air. André pulled his collar up around his neck as he and his fellow officers trudged through the fresh snow to their waiting railroad car. He was off to a land that he had only read about. He was only thirty-one and he wondered if he would celebrate many more birthdays. Reports from the front were sketchy at best. The Russian fleet had been badly damaged by Japanese torpedo boats. The harbor at Port Arthur was a mess of sunken ships and the Japanese had bottled up the Russian fleet.

The train sped along the rails with the incessant rhythm of the click clack, click clack that at times sounded like a distant machine gun firing in slow motion. An ominous sound, thought Yeshica, as he tried to sleep. If they were lucky and met with no mechanical problems, they would be well on their way to the front in less than two weeks. The First Siberian Regiment of Rifles had been blessed by the Tsar and now were enjoying a bit of the long trek before they would be tested in battle against the Japanese. How many would see their beloved homeland again before this was over?

André stood before Marshal Rosofsky and handed him a recent dispatch.

"Sit down, André," the Marshal said. "These reports are not good. The Japanese are moving troops to the peninsula faster than we can relocate our troops. If we did not have thousands of soldiers guarding the Trans-Siberian line to insure the safe movement of our regiments, we would be inviting a disaster. These Japanese are proving to be a crafty and brave lot. We have certain advantages against their army. We have an inexhaustible supply of cavalry. The Japanese are not good horsemen and they do not possess a lot of horses. We will have to use these advantages carefully when we engage them in battle."

"Sir", said André. "The Japanese artillery are proving to be excellent shots and their officers are extremely well educated in the scientific disciplines. Their guns are very mobile and have great range. This factor tends to somewhat equalize our cavalry superiority."

"You now see why I have you as an aide. Many of the ranking officers tend to listen to each other prattle on before they make up their minds. You might say they are testing the waters. No one wants to be left out in the cold when it comes to agreeing with the general staff. You always tell me straight away, André, and you are correct. We will not have an easy time of it. In numbers we have great strength. I expect 150,000 men in the field in the coming months. Our supplies are outstanding. We have the guns, ammunition, and foodstuffs to support our soldiers through many battles. Our men are brave and not afraid to die."

The train sped on. They were making excellent progress. Tomorrow they should be approaching Lake Baikal and the train and troops would be ferried across. Although a time consuming procedure, it had proven to be a doable, stopgap measure until the rail links could be completed.

As each day passed, more and more dispatches were received at the various stations along the route of the Trans-Siberian rail line. It was reported that Cossack regiments had encountered Japanese spies dressed as coolies whose aim was to sabotage the rail line and delay the movement of troops and supplies to the front.

They finally arrived at the bustling city of Harbin in one piece. The activity was horrendous. Cossack artillery regiments were racing south through the city to reinforce other units forming up to meet the advancing Japanese led by General Kuroki.

Marshal Rosofsky made his headquarters in one of the many beautiful homes that had been built by wealthy Russian industrialists who came to the area some years ago to develop the natural resources there. He sat at his desk wondering what was in store for the armies of Russia massing to the south. The silence was broken by a knock on the door." Come", he said. A young naval officer entered and handed him yet another dispatch.

"What news from Port Arthur?"

The young officer hung his head down and nearly started to sob." Admiral Makarov is dead. His ship encountered many mines laid down by the Japanese destroyers. The crew did not have a chance."

"This is a great loss for Russia, son". We will avenge his death. Do not despair. We will have our day and you will be there to see it."

André entered the room and escorted the naval officer, still distraught, from the room. He returned and addressed Marshal Rosofsky.

"Sir, the wounded are streaming into the city. We have suffered many casualties. We outnumbered the Japanese at the Yalu, but they outflanked us and made several bayonet charges until we were routed. They captured some of our older artillery pieces, but they have our soldiers in full retreat."

"We have definitely miscalculated the Japanese. Even though this is the first of many battles I am sure we will fight, it appears that the enemy has proven to be a match for our brave soldiers." said Marshal Rosofsky.

These were to be prophetic words over the next several months. Two more major battles at Kin Chou and Nan Shan Hill left both sides with many more dead and wounded but it was definitely a clear victory for the Japanese. The Tsar's description of them as little brown monkeys was coming back to haunt him. The Russians had fought bravely and fiercely against the enemy. The Japanese fought with extreme discipline and with great losses, but they were victorious.

André paused in the telling of his story. He wiped the sweat from his brow and repositioned the white, Panama hat on his head. The sun was still fairly high in the sky and, without any cloud cover, it was warm on the ramparts of the fort. Josh smiled at André and said, "Your memory of the events is amazing. I feel like I am there with my grandfather and you, and the only thing missing is the sound effects of the shells exploding."

"Those were sad days. I remember that as if it were yesterday. The dead; the dying; the wounded everywhere," said André.

"Did the Red Cross have a big role in taking care of the wounded?" Sarah asked.

"They were everywhere. There would have been many more dead if not for their heroic efforts."

"André," Marshal Rosofsky called out. André entered the room. "I have prepared a short statement for all military personnel and civilians in this area. I would like it read several times to insure that everyone gets the message. It is as follows:
It is with great sadness that I have to inform you that Mother Russia has lost one of her bravest sons. Admiral Makarov, pride of the navy and the Tsar's favorite, lost his life while giving chase to the Japanese fleet. His battleship hit several, uncharted mines, placed just outside the channel during the night.

Marshal Rosofsky, Special Envoy, to Tsar Nicholas II, Harbin Military District.

"I will see to it immediately," replied André.

"One more thing; get me a personal guard of ten men from the First Siberian Regiment. I will meet with General Kuropatkin who is moving up towards Mukden. That is where the next major encounter will occur. I want you to accompany me as usual. Colonel Libau will be in charge in my absence."

André saluted, did a smart about face, and left the room.

Mukden was not an old city. Built in 1625, before the Manchu's came to power, it had a traditional palace in the center of the city and several significant Tibetan monasteries. The inhabitants were mostly Chinese and numbered in excess of 250,000. A lull had occurred in the war, which was really no more than a short breather as Japan and Russian forces buried their dead from the last major battle at Liauyang and prepared to lock horns once again in the area in and around Mukden.

The armed guard of horsemen, bristling with rifles and sabers, galloped in the middle of the roadbed, passing many carts laden with all the worldly possessions of the refugees moving out of the outlying areas. It was always amazing how inhabitants of an area under assault were like flocks of birds before an oncoming storm. Somehow they knew that the winds would howl and the skies would open and bring forth torrents of rain and lightning. They sought shelter far from the storm well before it came.

CHAPTER 11

After several days of hard riding, the small entourage arrived at Mukden. During the time of China's governmental control, the city was called Shenyang.

The Tsar had given General Kuropatkin complete autonomy over the military forces fighting the Japanese. Marshal Rosofsky knew that he would have a difficult time convincing the General to change tactics in light of the gross miscalculation of the fighting men of Japan. But, he wanted to try, as the battle that loomed ahead would involve over a half a million soldiers and, if Russia was to win this one and turn the tide of the war, something additional, innovative, and daring was needed.

Nothing came out of the meeting. General Kuropatkin was determined that the might of Russia would prevail over the enemy. He made eloquent speeches to the troops and had the priests bless the men, hoping to shield them from harm by the strongest force known to man.

"André, give the men a break today," said Marshal Rosofsky. "I want to go to the field hospital set up at the Buddhist monastery and visit the wounded. I have quite a few St. George's Crosses to give out. Our Cossacks scouts have already encountered Japanese troops moving very close to the south of us. Tomorrow we will try and see what the Japanese troop movements are doing. So get some rest yourself," said the Field Marshal.

"As you wish, Sir," replied André. The Buddhist monastery was very old, almost as old as the city itself. The monks had come forward as the wounded streamed into the city and offered their temple to be used as a hospital along with the monks themselves giving aid and comfort to the wounded. Marshal Rosofsky met the head monk in charge at the monastery and marveled at the calm composure that exuded from him. He was gracious, wise and humble.

The monastery was filled with the wounded and the dying. Several Red Cross workers were seen to be everywhere as first one man called out and then, clear across the room, another screamed in pain. The spirits of the men were greatly uplifted to see such a high-ranking officer personally coming to see them.

Marshal Rosofsky, as military advisor to the Tsar, spoke from his heart when he said that the Tsar knew of the personal sacrifice of each and every man there.

He pinned the St. Georges Cross on the tunic of a soldier who had lost a leg and an arm. He spoke to the nurse.

"Will this man survive this trauma?"

"I doubt it. He has lost too much blood," she said

Marshal Rosofsky had seen death before but looking around the great room he was overcome with a wave of helplessness. Russian defeat here would not mean the end of Russia. Death would be the end for many in this place and, with the great battle looming just over the horizon in the days to come, he began to wonder about his own mortality and whether he would ever see his own son and wife again. He regained his composure and continued to pass out all the medals he had brought.

He encountered the head monk once again.

"This is a very old and magnificent monastery. Can I entreat you to show me around before I depart?" said the Field Marshal.

"It would give me great pleasure. I just wish that times were not so difficult," replied the monk.

Marshal Rosofsky walked about the great temple and marveled at the magnificent statues of Buddha. The head monk gave him a short history of the monastery and how it had survived, first under the Manchu's, and now under the Russians. He prayed that the monastery would survive the onslaught that was sure to envelope the whole city in the coming days.

Marshal Rosofsky stepped outside in the fresh air. He filled his lungs and felt his spirits rise. In spite of everything, it was a beautiful day.

On the street below the fort, Christos had read his paper twice. How much longer were they going to spend up there in the fort? What were they talking about anyway? Besides, tonight was card game night. The government did not own his soul even if they thought so. He was not some stunt actor from the movies. How close could he come to really scaring André Zommer without killing him?

André paused in his story long enough for Josh to ask him a question. "André, you said the Japanese were massing troops to the south of Mukden, or Shenyang, whatever they call that city. My grandfather was not an active combatant. You said he died in battle and you were with him," said Josh.

"I am getting to that my young friend. My mind is clear but give an old soldier a break. This happened sixty years ago.

André looked over at Sarah.

"I am sorry for the long story, my dear. It is something I have not spoken about for such a long time. It feels good to tell someone what happened, and especially, to Josh as I know it means so much to him."

"André, you really are a good story teller. Please continue," said Sarah.

"Yes, do continue, by all means," piped in Josh.

The following day, Marshal Rosofsky, André, and the small detachment of First Siberian Rifles left the city through the east gate and followed the sound of artillery fire to the south. A regiment of Cossacks could be seen in the distance with many Japanese prisoners. They stopped on top of a high promontory overlooking what was to become a major battlefield. André handed the Field Marshal a pair of binoculars.

"Look, there to the southwest, Sir. The Japanese are making a wide, sweeping, flanking movement. I do not see our troops," said André.

"They are probably moving through that valley a little to the north of them," replied the Field Marshal.

Just then, there was a tremendous flash of light and the sound of hundreds of cannons.

"I think the Japanese have spotted our army," said André.

Marshal Rosofsky could now see the soldiers running with their field packs. They were overloaded, like pack animals, with teakettles, pickaxes, and shovels besides their compliment of cartridge belts, and rifles. Where did General Kuropatkin think he was sending these soldiers, on an extended camping vacation? The Japanese were moving twice as fast, flanking the army in the valley as the Russian soldiers were trying to escape the fury of the artillery bombardment. But it was no use. The Russians were already routed. A group of officers were blasted from their positions not far from the front of the line and the soldiers started to run wherever they could to be free of the exploding shells.

The shells started to get closer to the small group standing on the hill.

"Get your men some cover over by those rocks," said André to the Sergeant Major." No need for all of us to have our heads blown off."

Now, other major units could be seen moving up the center pushing the Russians forward. At the same time, to the southeast, the Japanese had already flanked the Russian army and were tightening the noose as the soldiers ran headlong into the trap.

The smoke blotted out the sun as the small group watched in disbelief at the true horrors of war. The shrapnel from the shells had been most deadly. Thousands of dead and dying soldiers could be seen on the ground as the Japanese raced forward into the battle with bayonets fixed, like samurai of old.

As the shells got closer, the horses started to fidget and get nervous. They had been trained to know these sounds well, but they still did not like to hear it.

"We had better think about moving our position soon, Sir," said André.

"There is not much we can do for those poor souls down there."

Marshal Rosofsky turned his horse to face André.

"I would have done it differently. If only Kuropatkin would have taken my advice. We needed speed and mobility. What a loss. Stupidity, just plain stupidity."

Just then a high-pitched, whistle sound emanated from the sky. A series of shells started to rain in on the hill.

"The Japanese must have spotted us," yelled André over the deafening sound of the shells as they exploded in front of them. Damn, these Japanese were too damn accurate with their artillery."

Just then, a single shell landed within meters of Marshal Rosofsky. His horse bolted and reared on his hind legs, clawing at the deafening sound. The Field Marshal fell to the ground and his horse fell on top of him, having been struck by shrapnel right through the heart. Both horse and rider died instantly.

CHAPTER 12

André appeared to be exhausted from re-living the events he had just recounted for the past few hours. It was like old war wounds that had been opened and had salt poured on them. He was getting too old for this. These thoughts had not entered his mind for many years. But he was ninety and he hoped that this would be the last time he would relive this tale.

Josh sat on the stone wall in deep thought at what he had just been told. This was fantastic. To travel halfway around the world and meet someone who knew and served with his grandfather; who had been there when he died was too unbelievable. André appeared to be completely sincere. But, it was always possible that this was an old man's tale, a figment of his imagination.

"André, I do not know what to say! This is an utterly fantastic story"

"You can believe it. It is true, every word. It is as if it happened yesterday. I can hear the scream of the shells. I can hear the screams of the horses. I can feel the earth shudder beneath my feet," said André.

"André has a photographic memory," blurted Sarah.

"What happened after the battle?"

"The war is history. I dispatched an honor guard to take your grandfather back to his home in Kiev. I returned to Harbin and packed his personal belongings as we had done for so many others, and sent them and your grandfather home. I had to report to the Tsar the details of the events of the past few months and the death of his Field Marshal. Like I said, the war is history. The Russian Empire is history. The Tsar is history."

Josh could see that André was becoming melancholy and perhaps he had troubled the old gentleman long enough.

"I do not know how I can thank you for giving me these treasures about my family. You have given me so much of your time. Your kindness to me will never be forgotten. If there is anything, anything at all I can ever do for you, do not hesitate to ask," said Josh.

"In an odd way I have been repaid more than I can tell. The memory of your grandfather was highly valued by many in the government. His name opened many doors for me and when the revolution came and I was forced to flee or be shot like so many others, it was because of my close association with him that I received safe passage to Constantinople."

Christos sat in the car and watched the small group high up in the battlements. He was getting very impatient. The sun was starting to drop in the West and long shadows started to form from the huge walls of the fortress.

"I think it is time that we started back," said Josh.

"I want to walk along the Bosporus a ways," said André. "If you do not mind, I would like to be alone."

"Can I share a taxi with you, Josh?" asked Sarah.

"My pleasure," replied Josh.

The small group headed down the many stairs to the street level next to the

Bosporus. Josh stepped into the street to hail a taxi. André turned to Josh and said," I want to thank you for giving me the opportunity to tell someone, especially you, what a great man your grandfather was and how much I admired and respected him. Let us all have lunch once again before you leave Turkey."

"Good-bye," Josh said in parting. "Allahaismarladik."

"Gule, gule," responded André.

As a taxi approached to pick up Josh and Sarah, another car sped towards the small threesome as they started to split up and go their separate ways. There was more than enough room for the two vehicles to pass in the street. The black Citroen angled extremely close to the tall man dressed in a white linen suit with a white panama hat. At the last second, it swerved, hitting the old man, propelling him into the oncoming taxi.

"Dikkat, be careful" screamed Sarah.

It was too late. André bounced off the hood of the Citroen and was then crushed beneath the wheels of the taxi. The black sedan raced off at a high rate of speed, and one more accidental death was recorded in this city without traffic lights.

CHAPTER 13

Sarah screamed in horror at the sight of André being crushed beneath the wheels of the taxi. Josh raced to his side to help. But, André was dead before he hit the ground. Sarah wiped the blood from his face and closed his eyes.

Josh was the first to speak. "Those dirty bastards. They killed him. This is no accident. Someone wanted him dead. But why?"

Sarah recovered her composure and said, "He was deeply involved in many things. He was much more than he appeared to be."

Josh looked at her, "Sarah, I know that André helped our government from time to time, but why would they, and I think we are talking about the Russians, why would they want to kill him? He was an old man to say the least."

"I wish I knew. He has no family, only a very small circle of friends. He was always a very private person. I'll miss him."

"What will you do now, Sarah?"

"I am an Israeli, Josh. André also helped us from time to time, just like he helped your government. Maybe he knew too much and that is why they killed him. We probably will never know."

After André was cremated, a small service was held at a Greek Orthodox Church he had frequented. Josh was there with Gabe and Mary. Sarah and a few members from the college were there. Officially, the death was recorded as a hit and run and with so many black Citroens in Istanbul, it was highly doubtful the one that hit André would ever be located.

Josh said his goodbyes to Sarah, wishing that he could have spent more time with this beautiful, sensitive, woman. His mind was filled with so many new thoughts; he had to start somewhere and sort them out. He actually needed a long vacation. Maybe even a return home to Monterey.

Sarah, on the other hand, had her job to do. Her position as an assistant to a very special friend of Mossad, who had kept her government appraised of the entire goings on in Istanbul, had come to an end until a new source was found. She needed a vacation also. Maybe her boss would approve a leave for her and she could spend some time with this new, attractive diplomat who had appeared from nowhere and had stirred the blood in her veins.

Josh had a long meeting with Gabe. He told him André's story about his grandfather. He left out the part about whatever was given to his grandfather by the Tsarina.

"I've had no leave for several years," said Josh. "I really need some rest. I'm going to notify Washington that I am going home for thirty days and catch up on living."

Gabe looked into the tired eyes of his friend. These past few days could be seen in his face. He looked as if a heavy weight had been placed on his face like a mask. "An excellent idea, Josh. Your work here is done and I am sure the Department will grant you some well-deserved time off."

Just then the buzzer sounded." Sir, there is a lady on the phone for Mr. Ross."

"Who is it?"

"She said just to say Sarah."

"Put her through," as Gabe handed the phone to Josh.

"I am so glad I caught you, Josh. I am taking a special trip for the Israeli legation and am going to Los Angeles. Our government is trying to raise money to encourage the Russians to resettle Jews from the Soviet Union to Israel. It will take a staggering sum of money and I am going to work with a small delegation to spread the word about what and why this has to be done."

"I am planning a trip back also," said Josh. "My home is in Monterey. Maybe we can spend some time together. I really would like that if you have the free time."

"That would be wonderful," replied Sarah without hesitation.

"Please do call me at the legation office. I will be there until we feel our goal is accomplished. Just ask for Sarah Burstein"

"I am really looking forward to showing you some beautiful places in my neck of the woods, Sarah."

"Josh, l'hitraot."

CHAPTER 14

Colonel Sloven and Christos were meeting just as Josh was recounting his story to Gabe at the Consulate.

"You idiot, Christos, I told you not to kill the old fool, just to scare him."

"It was not entirely my fault, Comrade Sloven. The taxi came out of nowhere and crushed him under the auto just as I swerved to scare him."

"That is not what I heard, Christos. You were being watched by Novikov and Feodor from the Russian bureau and they called me and said you hit him squarely and pushed him into the taxi."

"Off the record, comrade, I will say that our comrades will say anything to protect themselves from their crazy boss Ivan Dzerzhinsky. I stand by my story. I swerved and he jumped out of the way into the path of the taxi which he did not see coming."

Sloven sat back in his chair and squeezed his chin and rubbed his eye.

"The Russians are reporting to Dzerzhinsky now and it will be the story I have just told you. I am afraid, comrade, that you have made a grave mistake that I cannot sweep under the rug. I have to clean this mess up quickly so that our Russian masters do not think we are incompetent. You will have to make a small sacrifice for the good of the organization."

Sloven quickly drew a Walther PP from his waistband and fired one shot straight into Christos' open mouth. The hole was small going in but the 9mm round blew the back of his head off. Sloven wiped his gun butt clean and placed it into the right hand of Christos, then placed the gun into his mouth. A guard from down the office corridor came running into the office. He opened his mouth to speak but Sloven put his finger to his mouth.

"Our comrade could not face the embarrassment of failure. He shot himself, as you see, before I could stop him. Get some help and see that my office is cleaned up."

It did not take long for word of Christos' death to reach the keen ears of the Russians. Novikov was on the phone with his superior in Moscow, Ivan Dzerzhinsky, grandson of the founder of the Cheka, Felix Dzerzhinsky and now one of the most feared policemen in the KGB.

"The incompetent fool who killed the old teacher has taken his own life rather than explain his failure. We should have taken care of this ourselves rather than leave it to the Bulgarians."

"The Bulgarians have their special place," replied Dzerzhinsky. "They do our dirty laundry well. But I am more interested in the dead teacher. I know that he helped the Americans. I want to know more about his last few days. Why was he meeting the American diplomat, Ross? I am sure he was not just showing him the ancient sights of the city. Your memorandums to me state that André Zommer was a Russian by birth. Find out when he came to Turkey and anything else in his background and get back to me as soon as possible. I will have my sources here track this diplomat Ross and see what his background is. Somehow, I have a gut feeling that there is a connection here that we are missing.

CHAPTER 15

It did not take long for Sloven to do what he was well trained for. He found out that André Zommer had come to Istanbul with other White Russians as a refugee from the aftermath of the Bolshevik revolution. He did not know that he was a former Russian officer in the army. He wasted no time in contacting Dzerzhinsky with what he had learned.

His Russian counterpart had also been busy. Fortunately, the Bolsheviks, when they came to power, did not destroy everything that had formerly been connected to the Tsarist Empire. All documents and information related to that former regime had been filed away in secret vaults, deep below the Kremlin.

André Zommer's name surfaced as one Andréyavich Zommer, a former Colonel and staff officer to none other than Field Marshal Yeshica Rosofsky. This field marshal of the Tsar's was often seen with the royal family and was a close advisor to the Tsar.

Dzerzhinsky sat at his desk and rubbed the pages in the file. What was it about this whole picture? A former Russian officer meets with an American diplomat.

What had they talked about? What could Zommer have told Joshua Ross?

Were the agents in Istanbul telling him all the details and why did the Bulgarians kill Zommer? This was becoming a real mystery.

He picked up the phone. "Get me my father at his dacha on the Black Sea."

A few minutes later the phone rang.

"How are you, Father? Are you getting plenty of fresh sea air and sunshine? I envy your opportunity to enjoy such leisure. But you have earned every minute of it."

"It is good to hear from you, son. But you are an important man now. To what do I owe the pleasure of your call?"

'Father, think back to some of the stories that grandfather used to tell you, especially those of the royal family at the time of the first war with Japan."

"My memory is not what it used to be, son. I know that your grandfather was obsessed with finding a long lost treasure of Russia that was last seen worn by the Tsarina at the time of the war."

"That would be the priceless necklace that you used to tell me about; the one that Peter the Great gave his wife Catherine. I thought we had obtained all those treasures from the royal family."

"We came to the conclusion that one of the guards watching the royal family stole it from the Tsarina. But we could never prove it and we never found it. Your grandfather spent many years looking, questioning people and frankly wasting a lot of precious time searching for this treasure."

"Father, I have come across the name of a dead field marshal, Yeshica Rosofsky, a close advisor to the Tsar. Does that ring a bell with you?

"I know what you know. I think he died in the war. What kind of goose chase are you involved in, son? "

"I do not know, Father. These names have surfaced after these many years and incidents have occurred that cannot be construed as coincidental. And we both know, in this business, nothing is ever coincidental. Call me in Moscow if you think of anything else."

CHAPTER 16

Josh caught the next Pan Am flight out of Istanbul. It was a great ride if you were a tourist. It would stop in Vienna, Frankfurt, and London, then to Washington. He figured he would make his final report to his boss, then take his much deserved vacation, including getting to know Sarah better.

He sat back in his seat, closed his eyes and thought about, of all things, how he had gotten this far in life. He remembered his childhood, which seemed so long ago: growing up in Southern California; his father working 12 hours a day as a plumber to send Josh to a good school in a good neighborhood; his mother, always there for him, but always doing part-time work to supplement the budget. Things were tough during the depression. She died of TB when he was in high school.

He finished high school and, much to his surprise, at the top of his class. His father was so proud of him. He wanted Josh to be well educated, something he never had an opportunity to do. Josh excelled in history and English and spoke fairly fluent French.

The roar of World War II was hard to muffle. Josh wanted to do his part and had always wondered what made those Marines look so confident and strong. Josh's father had no objections to him joining and gave Josh his blessing.

Camp Pendleton was not too far from home. He packed his bag, hopped a Greyhound and went to enlist. The Marines needed every good man they could find. He was in good health, could read and write, had a good pulse and a warm body. He learned to shoot a rifle, carry a 60 lb. pack on his back, climb up hills, crawl through lots of dirt and recognize a machine gun when he heard it.

It was not long before he was on a troop ship heading for the action in the many islands in the Pacific. Life as a Marine was very demanding. They used to tell him that he was better than any other soldier. And, when he was outnumbered ten to one it was considered a fair fight.

He did not like to remember those days. It was best kept a blur. What he did remember was when he thought he had lost his mind. It was one of the long days on Okinawa. The Japanese had this little island north of the big island and their planes were attacking our troops during the invasion. The brass had focused on the invasion and did not need this side distraction. They dispatched a small group to see if they could destroy the runway and take the pressure off.

Josh was part of that group and during the mission a Japanese pillbox with heavy machine gun fire pinned them down. Several of his buddies were literally cut in half. It was hard to think clearly with men falling dead all around you. Josh charged the enemy position, knowing only that he had to silence that machine gun before they all were killed. A handful of grenades did the trick. His lieutenant called him a hero. Josh was awarded the Silver Star for that action. He never felt he had deserved it. His friends who had died that day deserved it more than he. He felt he had done what he was supposed to do and what he was trained to do; nothing more, nothing less.

When we dropped the atom bomb and the Japanese cried "Uncle", it was finally over. Josh was asked if he would like to be part of the Marine Guard in Tokyo. It sounded interesting, so he accepted. Tokyo was a busy place. Our military was running everything while our government was trying to establish a new democratic way of life for the Japanese. Josh met a lot of the brass while he was there. He was befriended by a man and his wife whom he had met at Friday night services. The man was a top aide to one of the generals. Josh got a lot of advice from this gentleman and he suggested that Josh think about working for the State Department. Of course, he would have to go to college and get top grades to be considered. But, if he did well, his friend said, he would be his sponsor and see that he got a good start. Josh studied hard at night and during his off time, and by the time his tour was up, he had amassed many college credits through correspondence courses. He went to UC Berkeley summer and winter and in two and a half years, he was a magna cum laude student.

Josh was awakened from his reverie by the sound of the wheels on the big jet touching the runway. He looked out the window to see Vienna's terminal in the distance. After deplaning, he found a comfortable spot at the bar in the terminal and continued to reminisce about his getting into the Foreign Service and his

good fortune of rapid advancement to this
time in his life.

CHAPTER 17

After André's small funeral, Sarah filed her report to her superiors in Israel, leaving many unanswered questions regarding his death. She felt there was a definite connection between André's murder and the meetings with Joshua Ross. She emphasized the need to follow this up due to the sketchy story of André, relative to the death of Field Marshal Rosofsky. She was directed to pursue this in conjunction with her refugee fund raising efforts in Los Angeles.

On the other side of town there was a heated meeting between the Russians and the Bulgarians. Sloven now wanted to share his newfound information with Novikov and Feodor.

"That sure is a lame story about Christos shooting himself," boasted Novikov.

"Believe it, or don't believe it. You know the rules in our business. There is always someone to blame for failure. Today it is Christos. Who knows, tomorrow it may be you."

"Dzerzhinsky is not satisfied. He knows that Zommer was a former officer who served with Field Marshal Rosofsky. He did not get to be who he is and where he is by believing in coincidences. He wants all three of us to get to the bottom of this and he does not care if we have to travel halfway round the world to do it. So Sloven, get your Russian passport in order. You are now officially working for me as a trade delegate and as soon as we can we are off to a capitalist trade convention in Los Angeles, California. Any questions?"

"What about a weapon?" said Sloven.

"We will get those things from our contacts in Los Angeles. No need to raise a red flag as to who we really are." said Feodor.

As Josh finished his drink at the bar, he heard the boarding announcement for the continuation of his flight to Frankfurt. It was a shorter flight then the last leg and the big jet rolled in to Frankfurt right on time. He made his connection to Washington and after a long nap and a good dinner; he could see the U.S. coast as they broke through the clouds.

Going home always gave Josh a warm feeling. He could not put his finger on it, but it was there. The people, all speaking his native tongue, the big highways, with fast moving flashy cars, or the feeling that he did not have to look over his shoulder to see who was following him.

He went through the customary de-briefing. Said hi to many of his colleagues, and signed out for a long overdue vacation. He kept the story of his meeting with André Zommer and his "accidental" death to himself. No need to raise flags yet. The transportation department advised him that, if he hurried, he could catch a KC135 going to Travis Air Force Base just east of San Francisco. From there it was a short ride down the coast to Monterey and home.

CHAPTER 18

In California, if you get it right, the sun is always warm and the air is cool. He could feel the sun on his face and, with the top down on his rental Mustang, he knew he was home. Highway 101 South was the road there. As he approached Gilroy, he could smell the garlic miles away. He was close. He made his turn at Highway #68 and, soon, he was breezing by Laguna Seca Raceway. He loved this place. He belonged to a sports car club and whenever he was home he would get out his four-wheel treasure and do a few laps on the track. His club, of course, paid for the privilege, but it was worth it.

Josh lived just across from the Navy Post Graduate School on Sloat. It was nothing fancy; a two-bedroom apartment, which he owned, and a one-car garage. Being on the road so much, he often felt he should rent out the place. But, being that the apartment and his car were his only worldly possessions, he wanted it to be his, and only his.

Josh had only been home a short while before there was a knock on the door. To his surprise, it was his neighbor, George Boer.

"Hey, Josh, welcome back, we missed your smiling face around here. I've been starting your car weekly and making sure no things decided to make it their home."

"I really appreciate that, George. You're a good friend."

"You have to take me out to the track, Josh. I bet you can give the track record a run for its money "said George.

"Not quite, but it will really hump."

Josh was referring to his 1958 Porsche Carrara Speedster that he'd brought back from Stuttgart. Even though it was far from new, it had been hardly driven. But Josh was going to change that real soon.

"I really appreciate you looking after it while I am away. You certainly deserve a run around the track," said Josh."

Josh used George's phone to call the phone company, and no sooner was it back in service, than its familiar ring sounded throughout the apartment.

Now what? thought Josh.

It was his boss in Washington. "Yes Sir, I'm home. What's up?"

"Josh, I have a real plum for you if you're interested. It will give you a break, also. We've pushed you hard these past two years. Whenever we asked you to do something, you did it well, without a lot of direction."

"Well, thank you, sir, for your confidence,"

"Josh, how would you like to teach a course at the Navy Post Graduate School? You would have to come up with the curriculum, but it would be like "Diplomacy for Dummies". With your many years of experience and your track record, I think you could really teach those young officers a thing or two that they could not get from a textbook."

This was too good to be true, thought Josh. It would fit in perfectly with his seeing Sarah more and give him some time to research the information he had received from André regarding his grandfather.

"I accept your fine offer without reservation," replied Josh.

"It's done then. I'll make a few calls and secure all the paperwork. I'll be in touch. Oh, one more thing. I almost forgot. We received a communiqué from Gabe Smith in Istanbul asking about you and if we had an address where he could reach you".

"Of course, by all means, he is like family to me."

'Good luck to you, and we know we'll only hear good things about you from the Navy."

Josh walked through the kitchen to the garage door. He flipped on the garage light and stared at his Porsche, all covered up. Removing the cover, he fondly stroked its silver finish. First, I'm going to have you serviced by Helmut, my favorite German mechanic, he thought. Then a deluxe polish job and you'll be ready to hit the road. Maybe a quick trip to L.A. to see how Sarah was settling in, and tell her about his good fortune of being able to, hopefully, stay in California for a year.

CHAPTER 19

The Jewish Federation of Los Angeles was thrilled to hear of Israel sending a representative to direct the program to help spur the move of Russia's Jews to Israel. Sarah was thrilled, too, as it would give her an opportunity to see Josh, even for a short while, before he was back on his job. She also had her instructions to follow up on the story she had heard from her former colleague about Josh's grandfather.

Sloven, Feodor and Novikov had already landed in Washington and were being briefed at their Embassy by the Intelligence Chief.

"You are to have no physical contact with this Ross fellow. You are to follow him, report on whom he sees and talks to.

We would be very pleased if you can plant a bug in his home. Keep us advised of your success; we are not interested in your failure. Your cover will be as representatives to the trade show and we will supply you with other technical and trade opportunities to give you sufficient cover after the convention is concluded. You have your contact in L.A. who will supply you with anything else you might need. This is not a vacation and rubles are still scarce, so mind your business and do your best. Dzerzhinsky himself will be monitoring your progress. He believes that this Ross was given some vital information before the teacher was killed in Istanbul. We want to know what it is."

The speech concluded, the three "spies" took a deep breath and filed out of the office.

"Like we were a bunch of amateurs," said Sloven.

"Mind your tongue. You will follow orders just like Feodor and I."

"I am a Bulgarian agent and a dammed good one. I will not be spoken to like a school boy," said Sloven.

"You are now a Russian with a Russian passport and do not forget that," said Novikov.

The car came back from Helmut's shop with Helmut personally delivering it to him. "That Porsche is one sweet ride, Josh," he said. "Can you run me back to the shop?"

"No problem, it will let me see how the car runs."

Just then, the telephone rang, interrupting them. It was the Navy Postgraduate School. They had a special delivery via courier for Josh to pick up and sign for.

The car ran as smooth as silk through the gears and the clutch was perfect. It revved to 7,000 rpm with ease. Helmut had done a great job.

Josh pulled into the guest parking lot at the hotel. The school was, in addition, a real hotel that had been acquired by the Navy many years ago as a facility to house and train officers. It still was a magnificent building, with a wonderful dining room and many outlying classrooms for the school.

In the Commanding Officer's office, he introduced himself to the secretary. She directed him to the intelligence section where he would obtain his delivery.

"Josh Ross to see the Navy courier," he stated.

He signed for a large envelope, thanked the staff and drove back to his apartment. Slitting the heavy seal on the envelope, he found a letter from Gabe Smith.

The letter was quite interesting. Josh had no idea that he'd created such a stir with the Russians in Istanbul. He somehow knew that André had been murdered, but did not know that he had been under surveillance.

Gabe told him that three known agents had gone missing in the City according to the resident CIA agent in charge, He gave Josh their names and enclosed three 8x10" glossies of each one. He said that they had been clocked into Washington very recently and might show up in California.

Josh was on vacation, but he wanted to get a heads up on the course he had to put together at the postgraduate school. He spent several days in the library ordering some material from the vast resources of the State Department. In the evening, he focused on the last words of André over and over in his mind. Something of value, something of value, what could it be? Josh decided to call Sarah. Hopefully, she would be settled in and have a free weekend to be with him. He called, but had to leave a message. She was there, but out meeting with several organizations. He decided to surprise her. He wanted to take a long drive in his car anyway. Why not a fast run down the coast highway through Big Sur, past Hearst Castle and through Malibu, and then the big city.

He left that Friday after securing a pager from Navy communications.

He would stay in touch. The day was just beautiful. He put the top down on his Porsche and his foot down on the gas. The car was like a roller skate glued to the road. He took each curve and hill as fast as he dared. Not a lot of traffic, he thought. In a standard piece of Detroit iron this road was strictly for tourists. If you missed a curve going too fast, you could wind up over a cliff into the Pacific. On the other hand, his Porsche was designed for this type of driving and loved the challenge.

CHAPTER 20

Sarah was completely surprised and overjoyed to see him. She gave him a tremendous hug and a bigger smile. Needless to say, Josh responded in kind. They drove out to Santa Monica for dinner and sat outside at a café. "I have some wonderful news for you," he said. "I am going to teach a course for a year at the Navy Post Graduate School. I live right across the street from it and it really will be a treat for me. And you can come up and visit as I have an extra bedroom. Of course, that is, if you really want to."

"What a question. Of course I want to and I do not think the extra bedroom will be necessary." She delivered those words with an even bigger smile.

"Sarah, I felt the same way from the very first time we met. I knew there was an attraction but I've been a loner so long I was hesitant to say anything. I'm not a youngster anymore and I'm a little set in my ways."

"I agree with you, to a point. Each case is different. I have been away from home for several years. Any attachments I would have liked to have are long gone. André was a wonderful person, but he was more a grandfather to me. I did not date any Turkish men and I will not even go into that subject."

Josh told Sarah about the letter from Istanbul. He showed her the pictures of the three agents and they discussed the ramifications. Sarah was very candid. She told him that she also was mystified by André's story and would like to work with Josh to solve the mystery, find André's killer and put this to rest. She told Josh that her work would also take her to San Francisco, just up the road from Monterey. If they needed more time to solve the mystery, she was sure she could get permission to stay on. She said her superiors also were concerned about the death of their trusted friend, who had done innumerable things for them.

"In a few weeks," he said, "there will be a whole week of antique car shows and auto racing at Laguna Seca. The Pebble

Beach show alone is a blast and it will be an opportunity to meet some very big givers to your cause. You have to be wealthy to own a car worth a half a million. You can spread your message to people who have big hearts and the means to help in a big way."

Novikov and his two comrades had been very busy. They found a cheap motel to stay in, which really was an upgrade from their place in Istanbul. Hot water all the time. They found out where Josh lived, but did not find out about his teaching assignment. Two of them would watch Josh, while the third would go through the motions at the trade shows.

Their hiatus gave Josh and Sarah time to be alone together without someone looking over their shoulder. It was a wonderful weekend and they both realized that, if at all possible, they wanted to spend as much time together as their work allowed. Josh drove home with love looking over his shoulder. On Josh's return to Monterey, he noticed the Pacific Power and Light truck parked near his apartment. Once inside his home he found that he had no electricity. Now what, he thought. He stepped outside and hailed the man sitting in the truck.

"What gives?" The fellow looked at him rather oddly and then looked at a clipboard on the dash.

"It says here that there was a request for increased power lines to your unit for a ham radio broadcasting system. Is that right?"

"I never ordered any such line," replied Josh.

"Beats me, I will have to double check with my office. It is possible that I have a garbled address."

Just then, another man came out from around Josh's home carrying a black bag of tools and a spool of cable.

"The man says there was no order for more power line," said one worker to the other.

"The line is installed," said the man carrying the black bag.

"There is no charge to you for the work and you are only charged if you start using the extra power. So, if I were you I would just let it be," said the driver of the truck.

With that said the other man got into the truck and they drove away.

Josh thought this was all very bizarre. He did not suspect that he had just had his apartment bugged by some questionable amateurs.

Josh's vacation passed too quickly. He played some tennis at the courts nearby, walked to Fisherman's Wharf along the bay bike path and tried to come up with some way to unravel the mystery of what the old Russian had told him. Before he realized it, the big weekend of the car shows was upon him. He called Sarah and asked her to come up about the middle of the week so she could see some of the warm up races at Laguna Seca race track and then they would take in the Pebble Beach Tour d' Elegance on that Sunday. She was all for that and left Josh in a wonderful frame of mind.

Sloven and Feodor sat in the Chevy sedan not far away on Josh's street.

"I think we are wasting our time up here," said Sloven.

"So far so much drivel. He likes to play tennis and takes walks. He does not seem to even own a camera. He likes cars and ladies. So do I."

"Sloven, you are never going to learn. You have to follow orders. Our orders are to monitor everything this fellow does regardless. In other words, we are not being paid for our opinions. I would not want to get on the wrong side of Dzerzhinsky."

"I hear you, but I still say this fellow does not appear to have any plans to follow. He would have done something already if there was anything to do with the old teacher. I say we are wasting our time," said Sloven.

"I will call Novikov and advise him of our progress. I know he will not be happy," replied Feodor.

CHAPTER 21

Sarah arrived during the middle of the week at the local Monterey airport. She looked radiant and Josh felt like a million dollars with her sitting by his side, she was a keeper. She loved his apartment and said it was twice as big as some of the units in Israel.

"There are some great restaurants here in town, fish, lamb, beef whatever is your pleasure."

"I love fish."

"Fish it is then. I know a place on the wharf with great atmosphere and we can sit outdoors and listen to the sea lions sing."

The night with Sarah was more than he expected. She was vibrant and full of energy. Waking in the morning with her still in his arms, convinced him that he was not going to let this one get away, no matter what.

The next day, they hopped into his Speedster and headed for Laguna Seca. The practice runs had already started and drivers were gearing up and tuning up their cars for the historic races to be held that weekend.

Josh, being a member of the Sports Car Club, was able to get into the paddocks where all the cars were berthed. There were Jags of all years, a multitude of Porsches, MGs, Alfa Romeos, historic Bugattis and even a few Bentleys and Ferraris. Josh enjoyed engaging the drivers in small talk about their cars and never hesitated to mention his Porsche Carrera.

After watching the cars whiz around the track for a while, they decided to head for town to see the cars that would be put on the auction block. Some of the Ferraris were going for close to a million dollars. The crowds of people were everywhere and Josh heard that all the hotel rooms were full. It was a real happening and he and Sarah were a part of it.

The Pebble Beach Tour d'Elegance on Sunday was the best of the best. The cars there were some of the most expensive ever made. Josh wished that he could have the insurance premium money for one year that was paid to insure these beauties. The entrance fee was pricey but the money went to charity. Sarah and Josh enjoyed rubbing elbows with many of the owners, actors, and other celebrities. The Rolls-Royces were everywhere, but their favorite was a baby blue Packard roadster.

Toward the evening, Sarah pulled Josh aside and told him of the wonderful time she had. Unfortunately, she had to go to Washington in a few days and could not stay any longer.

"Sarah, this is great. I have to go to the Library of Congress to do some research for the course I'm going to teach. I can drive you back to Los Angeles and fly out with you. We can spend some time together in Washington."

"That would be wonderful. I'd love to go to the Smithsonian if we have time," she said.

"We'll leave first thing in the morning."

Sloven and Feodor had a difficult time keeping up with Josh and Sarah. Not that they did not enjoy the car races and the car shows. They were professional enough to keep from being spotted and they were quite certain that the couple did not suspect their presence as yet. It would be only a matter of time before they knew they were being followed.

Josh and Sarah left that morning. Their bags were thrown in the little cubby area behind the seats. The top was down and they looked forward to a delightful drive down the coast highway that Josh thought of as his own personal track.

The two spies followed behind in their non-descript Chevy. There was a little traffic and they hoped they would not be spotted.

Josh brought the little silver bullet up to a comfortable speed a little over the speed limit and headed south. He had not forgotten about Gabe's warning.

"Sarah, please keep an eye on the rear view mirror for me. Those agents from Istanbul could be in California and, if they are here, then they surely know where I live. I am no big secret in the scheme of things."

As they headed further along the coast, the traffic started to thin. Josh increased his speed and focused completely on the hills and curves, which now were quite numerous.

At the same time, several miles behind, Sloven, who was driving, had a hard time keeping up with the little Porsche. The big Chevy swayed on its soft suspension and the average quality tires started to squeal on the curves. More and more the silver blur up ahead got further and further away.

"Josh, I see a dark sedan a ways behind us that seems to be all over the road. He is either drunk or a very poor driver. He has no idea of the limits of that car he is driving."

"Sloven, please do not kill us. I have the woman's name. We will check her out and see whom she is associated with in Los Angeles. They will not be too far ahead of us. We cannot keep up with that Porsche," said Feodor.

"I cannot buy that," replied Sloven. 'If we lose them, you know who will tear us limb from limb. Just hang on and bear with me." He mashed the pedal harder and the big lumbering sedan shot faster down the twisty road.

Josh, a few miles ahead was now flying low down the coast road. The surrounding sand dunes and cliffs were becoming a blur as the little car accelerated faster and faster. Sarah started to wince on some of the curves, but the car seemed to be glued to the road and no amount of thrashing would break it loose.

"Josh, please be careful. I know you are a good driver, but."

Sloven, who had now maxed out the speed of the big car was, literally, driving down the middle of the road. They were approaching the Rocky Creek Bridge and were going much too fast. Sloven had the good sense to slow somewhat, but braking too hard caused the big car to swerve even more.

As the road began to twist and turn, Sloven, to his horror, suddenly realized he had completely lost control of his ability to keep the car on the road. The Chevy hit the guardrail, bounced back to the road, and hit the cliff on the opposite side of the road, before rolling over and coming to rest on the only clear patch of dirt before the cliff dropped off to the ocean below. Feodor was thrown against the windshield smashing his skull to a bloody mess. Sloven was thrown from the car and by some miracle landed back on the road rather than being thrown over the cliff. Sloven, lay there, shaking all over. He finally raised himself up and walked to the car, limping as he went.

Feodor was dead. His face was hardly recognizable. Sloven, who was no stranger to death, shrugged his shoulders and thought; maybe they will give him a medal for his services. He was a good Russian.

Josh, with Sarah by his side, raced down the coastal highway completely unaware of the event that had just played out several miles behind them.

To their good fortune, they would benefit greatly as their adversaries numbers dwindled. It would take Sloven half a day to extricate himself from the accident investigation and return to his location in Los Angeles. In that time, Josh and Sarah would be well on their way to Washington and Sloven would not be any the wiser. His report to Novikov would implicate Feodor as the cause of the accident and exonerate himself.

CHAPTER 22

L.A. Airport was bustling with activity as Sarah and Josh arrived. They checked their baggage and went to the departure lounge. Waiting for the boarding call, they could not help but hear the lounge TV broadcasting news of the terrible accident on the coast highway the day before.

"We were there." said Sarah. "It must have happened a few miles behind us. Listen, they are saying the man was a foreign tourist and not familiar with the twisting highway of the coast. Do you think it could have been our Russian friends?"

"It's possible," said Josh. "I'll have my sources see if they can get more details once we get to Washington." The boarding call came and the two settled into their seats for the long flight.

Once in the nation's capital, Josh and Sarah agreed to meet that night, kissed, and went their separate ways.

At the State Department, Josh checked in to say hello, procured a list of literature and other information he needed, and then ducked out to head to the Library of Congress. Once there, he went to the general reading room and researched the books he felt would be useful for his upcoming diplomacy course. He was always impressed with the size and scope of the largest library in the world. It seemed that everything in print was sure to be found here.

He then went to the European Reading Room. He wanted to find out more information about his grandfather. He asked the librarian if there were any directories on Russian Generals and Field Marshals going back to the late 18th century. They had everything. Apparently, early in the 1900's, the Russian government contracted with a German organization to prepare a directory of just such a list of officers.

"I have exactly what you want," said the librarian. "Which officer are you interested in?"

"The name is Yeshica Rosofsky."

"In Russian, that R would be a P," replied the librarian. Then, looking puzzled, he said, "That's interesting, the directory ends with the start of the Ps. Let me check the printer's footnotes.

"You are out of luck, sir. It seems this body of work was unfinished at the time the First World War broke out. The work was stopped and never resumed since Germany and Russia were at war. Give me your name and where you can be reached and I will do some additional research on this. I cannot promise anything. When the Soviets came to power the flow of information came to an abrupt halt. It has been very difficult to obtain historical information, especially information from the era of the Tsars."

Josh thanked him and then asked,

"Do you have anything written on the Russo-Japanese War of 1905? I am interested in any detail that might have been written by eyewitness reports."

"Let me check the card catalogue. I do not get many requests for that, but if my memory serves me, there were many reporters from around the world who converged on the Manchurian Peninsula to cover the war. Newspaper accounts were quite numerous and they were compiled in a booklet."

He found the card and located the document. It was quite a complete coverage of many of the battles and politics, which occurred at the time.

Josh was most interested in the battle of Mukden where André had told him his grandfather had been killed. Sure enough, it was all there in fairly decent detail. The Russians had been routed in that battle and there had been a great loss of life on both sides. After reading the detail, he felt somewhat drained. André had given an excellent rendition of the events. Josh felt reassured by André's story. The old man had to be telling me the truth, he thought to himself. Now, if he could only figure out the other part.

CHAPTER 23

Sloven returned to Los Angeles nursing a traumatized body and leg. His report to Novikov was sketchy at best. He pleaded he did not remember exactly what had happened, since it had happened so quickly.

"I am going to have a hard time explaining this to Dzerzhinsky. In addition, you have lost surveillance on the man and the woman. Call her office and tell them you are from some charity that wants to donate money to her cause. Ask where she is, tell them you want to speak with her. Find out where she went. They are probably still together," said Novikov.

"That is exactly what I was going to suggest."

Three thousand miles away, Sarah was briefing her superiors at the Israeli Embassy. They were most interested in what Josh had discovered since leaving Istanbul. Other than that the Russians were shadowing them, there really was not a lot to tell. They told her to continue her association and learn as much as she could.

Josh called Sarah that afternoon and suggested they have dinner at the Old Ebbets Grille, an old, wonderful restaurant with superb steaks.

"Josh, I just found out that there is a marvelous show at the Smithsonian. They have on display fabulous jewels from all over the world, even the Louvre has sent over some of the crown jewels that Napoleon gave to Josephine."

"I'm finished with what I came to do. If you are also, we can go first thing tomorrow. Stay with me tonight at my hotel, I'm at the Ritz Carleton and it is first class. They give diplomats a discount."

Dinner was great and they were in the company of many of the most powerful and influential people in the United States. Old Ebbets Grille was legendary for that. The evening with Sarah was a pure delight and it only made Josh more determined to be with her always.

The next morning, after an early breakfast in bed, they were on the way to the museum. They arrived early, before the crowds began to form. The jewel displays were magnificent. So many museums had contributed to the show. They went from one to another, each one seeming to out glitter the next. They came to the crown jewels of Napoleon. The emerald and diamond necklace was one of the most beautiful pieces of jewelry they had ever seen. Sarah could not believe that there were emeralds that size.

Then appeared the most unusual exhibit. All by itself, there stood any empty display cabinet. The people of the Soviet Union had presented it. On the empty, silk stand appeared a short statement.

Coronation necklace of Catherine 1 given to her by Peter the Great in 1724. Worn by Alexandra, last Tsarina of Russia. Believed to have been stolen by her Bolshevik guards during her incarceration.

On the side was a photograph of Alexandra wearing the necklace.

Josh stood in front of the display for the longest period of time, as if transfixed. Sarah touched his elbow gently.

"Josh, what is wrong?"

"I don't know"

"What are you thinking?"

"I am remembering what André told me. He said, something of great value. The Tsarina and her family died in 1917. The family had many jewels sewn into their clothing, but there never was evidence of the whereabouts of the necklace of Catherine I. I may be totally off base, but I am thinking that, maybe, just maybe, this is what the Tsarina Alexandra gave to my grandfather for safekeeping. What are your thoughts?"

"I, too, remember André's exact words. You may have hit on it. So, after your grandfather left St. Petersburg and the Tsarina, he had the necklace in his possession. He had it with him until his death. But, it was not found among your grandfather's personal effects when André gathered them up and shipped them home with the body."

"You have a fabulous memory, Sarah. I think we are getting somewhere with this. Yesterday, I reviewed a document containing newspaper reports of the battle in Mukden where my grandfather was killed. So, at some point between the time he arrived at his headquarters in Harbin and his death near Mukden, he did something with the necklace."

"Do you think he would have entrusted it to anyone at his headquarters?"

"Not something of that great value and importance."

"But, he did do something with it."

"I agree with you, Sarah. Our focus has to be on every word André told us. Something there will point us in the right direction, I am certain of it. With your sharp memory we should be able to put two and two together.

"Tomorrow, we should return to California. I have my class to prepare for and I am sure that you have your work, too.

"I have yet to hear about the details of the auto accident on the coast road. I'm thinking that someone is suppressing the information. The more I think about it, if it were the Russians, they would do exactly that. The driver and passenger of that car must have been our two watchdogs. They tried to keep up with me and crashed," said Josh.

"I have not seen anyone resembling the pictures you showed me in Monterey. We are very fortunate that no one has followed our movements in Washington. Our trip to the museum is our secret. Let us keep it that way. If we can positively prove at least to ourselves that it was the necklace, then we can proceed to determine what your grandfather did with it," said Sarah. "I do not mean to be so long winded about this, but I love a good mystery and I think that is exactly what we have going for us."

"I'm going to have my office dig a lot deeper on the auto accident. I'll have them track the passports of the three. The FBI should be aware of the location of all foreign diplomats in the U.S., especially Russians," said Josh.

"I will need to check in at the embassy. Afterwards, I will come to your hotel and we can have dinner together."

"That sounds wonderful, Sarah. Until then."

Sloven was up against a blank wall. His anonymous call to Sarah's employer gave him little concrete information. All the person knew was that Sarah had mentioned that she would be with friends for the weekend, and maybe a little longer, but that she would be in touch. Sloven did not leave a call back number. On a hunch, he went to the airport and drove around the airport-parking garage. He knew there were not that many silver Porsche Speedsters around and he just might get lucky. After a full day of looking, he finally spotted the car. It was parked away from the rest and had been enclosed in a car cover. By then, the weekend was just about over and Sloven still had no idea where Josh had gone. After talking with Novikov, it was decided that Sloven would keep an eye on the car, waiting for its owner to return. He was to wait several days, which did not improve his temperament one bit.

CHAPTER 24

On their return to California, Sarah continued with her fund raising and the spreading of her message to as many organizations and groups as she could. Even the non–Jewish groups were interested as there was a sincere belief that it was necessary for an established Israel before the Messiah would come.

Josh returned to Monterey and the beginning of his class on diplomacy. He now conducted all his activities with the attitude that he must constantly be looking back over his shoulder. He did not know that his apartment was bugged, but he conducted his conversations as if it might be.

He spoke with Sarah on a regular basis, but due to their heavy work schedules they were not able to rendezvous, as he would have liked.

Josh had an assistant do some research on the coronation necklace. It was difficult, as information was hard to come by. The Tsarina had worn the necklace at many state functions early in the 1900's. Once the riots started and the Tsar's family had removed themselves from the public eye, it had never been seen again. It was anyone's guess when it disappeared. Josh could not decide whether he was back to square one or not. He continued to hope that his hunch was right and it was the necklace that had been entrusted to his grandfather when he left for the war.

Sloven maintained his vigil now, accompanied by Novikov. Ross had exhibited no outward signs of anything unusual. If he was doing something other than teaching, it was hard to determine.

"Why do we always wind up with the teachers," said Sloven. "This fellow is actually becoming boring."

Dzerzhinsky, himself was beginning to wonder if he was wasting his manpower and budget on the goose chase that his father had referred to. He decided he would give it another month before recalling the dogs.

CHAPTER 25

Sarah contacted Josh and told him that she was moving her activities to the San Francisco area. She would be much closer to him and they would be able to be together a lot more. They decided to meet the following weekend and tour the Monterey Aquarium.

The aquarium housed a world-class exhibit of some of the finest sea life in the oceans. It was a major attraction in Monterey and, besides the multitude of tourists, marine biologists from all over the world came to do research.

Sarah arrived early afternoon on Friday. After an excellent dinner and a walk along the wharf, they returned to Josh's place for the night.

In the morning, Josh suggested a game of tennis.

"Josh, I have not played tennis in years. I will be a terrible match for you. It will not be enjoyable for you."

"Don't be silly. I would love to teach you. You certainly are athletic and I think that you'll do very well once you get started."

Sarah thoroughly enjoyed the volleying and Josh told her the next time they played she would be ready for a match. They had a quick lunch at home, then headed for the Aquarium.

It was such a beautiful day; they decided to walk, as the Aquarium was not far from Fisherman's Wharf. The bike path they walked on was crowded with people. There were walkers, joggers, bicyclists, and skate boarders, all vying for the same small space on the path. They arrived at the Aquarium after a few close calls with a bicycle and a skate boarder.

Once inside the huge building, Sarah was amazed at the size of the tanks. She felt as if she had been transported to the ocean bottom and was gazing at a habitat few had ever seen. There were huge stingrays and all kinds of sharks. Turtles also were visible everywhere. The color and size of the tropical fish were just amazing. Each exhibit seemed to outdo the next. There were special exhibits for children that allowed them to touch the sea creatures. The children seemed to have a wonderful time with this. The time passed too quickly and, soon, Sarah had to say her good-byes.

Sarah invited Josh to San Francisco for the High Holy Days. She told him that she was not very observant but still liked to go to temple during this time. They made some plans and kissed, longingly goodbye.

Sloven and Novikov enjoyed the Aquarium also. Nothing like this where they lived. They kept their distance behind the couple and tried to blend in with the other foreign tourists.

The days passed quickly and, as the Holidays approached, Josh began to feel anxious about Sarah.

CHAPTER 26

Josh remembered that his father had passed away close to the time of the Holidays. He knew that it was very important to get the Hebrew date so that he could match it to the calendar. He had his assistant research that and, sure enough, it fell over the same period. I will bring my father's prayer shawl and use it for the services, he thought. That would be most fitting.

He had not used the tallit that his father had left him since he passed away. It was not that he had not attended any services; it was just that he had been away so much. This time would be different; he would do it right.

He began to search his apartment for his tallit. After an hour of searching, he knew he would have to do some reorganizing. Nothing seemed to be where it was supposed to be. He wondered if other people had as much trouble at finding things as he did.

Finally, buried deep in a bunch of clothes that he no longer wore on a regular basis, he found what he was looking for. It was a beautiful bag and the prayer shawl was safely inside, still folded neatly. He put the bag into his Hartman suitcase and finished packing for the few days he would spend in San Francisco.

He decided to drive up through Santa Cruz and Half-Moon Bay. He had not been there for several years. Once again, it was a beautiful day and his little silver car was very appreciative of the exercise.

As he sped along, the scenery was just magnificent. He wondered why more people did not appreciate the California ambience. Perhaps it was the crowded populace in the cities or maybe the fast rising taxes. Whatever the case, he was glad that, today, the roads were fairly free of cars. Soon, he would be approaching the megatropolis of San Francisco with all of its charm.

Sarah had been made a guest of one of the more wealthy families in the city.

She had been given a guesthouse cottage all to herself on the large compound and was very comfortable. She invited Josh to stay with her. She had told her sponsor that Josh was a diplomat which really smoothed the way.

The restaurants in San Francisco were legend. There were so many to choose from among all the ethnic cuisines. They had breakfast, lunch and dinner out until they thought they could not eat another morsel.

The next day coincided with the anniversary of his father's death and they attended services. They went to an old, established, conservative temple in San Francisco and sat together in the back of the sanctuary. The service was traditional and beautiful. Sarah, who was far more secular than Josh, enjoyed hearing the traditional melodies.

It came time for the Rabbi's sermon. Josh started to drift off, thinking about his father and how he would attend services with him when he was a little boy. He held his father's tallit bag in his hand and stroked its black velvet cover with a tender touch. It was truly a beautiful bag. He realized that this was the first time he actually had ever taken the time to examine it closely. Embossed with delicate embroidery, the bag looked a lot older than it actually was. He looked closer at the intricate design. It was scrollwork. There were two birds, a crown and some sort of design. It truly was beautiful.

Looking even closer, Josh could make out a date written on the bag, 1861. He gave a short gasp. This was his grandfather's tallit bag. His great grandmother must have made the bag for her grandson's bar mitzvah. At the top of the bag, in Hebrew, was the name Yehoshua Rosofsky. This, translated into Russian, was Yeshica, and in English, Joshua. His father had told him that he was named for his grandfather.

Sarah noticed Josh's shocked countenance.

"Is everything all right?"

"I have just made an amazing discovery," he said.

"Let's step outside and I'll tell you all about it."

Once outside, Josh showed Sarah what he'd just discovered and told her how thrilled he was. He actually held in his hands something his grandfather touched many, many, times during his life. It also must have been one of his personal possessions that André packed and sent back to Kiev with his grandfather's body.

He opened the bag and inspected the inside. It was as beautifully made inside as on the outside. He put his hand inside and felt the smooth fabric. At the bottom of the bag he felt a stiffness, different from the rest of the fabric.

"Sarah, put your hand in here. What do you feel?"

"It feels much stiffer than the other material. It feels like there is something under the fabric. Let's go back to the cottage and open this up very carefully and see what is there."

Back at the cottage, Josh used a razor blade to carefully slit the bottom seam. He was amazed at what he found; a piece of thin leather had been inserted in the bag and on the leather, still plainly legible, there were many rows of numbers and the design of a small black bird at the top.

A total riddle, thought Josh. "This has to mean something important. My grandfather had a good reason to place this here hidden in the bag."

"Obviously, it is some kind of code and the black bird is the key," said Sarah.

Josh studied the rows of numbers carefully. He tried to recall, back in his history studies, some of the old codes that were used by the French. His head started to throb from all the mental activity.

"Sarah, I can't do any more with this now. It's giving me a headache. I'll take this home and with the help of our crypto department, see if I can decipher these numbers. First, though, I have to determine what document these numbers refer to."

"Josh, I'm coming with you. I have extensive training in codes and I am sure that two heads will be better than one. I feel certain that the black bird at the top of the numbers is the key to the puzzle. I'll try to help you remember something that your father may have told you that relates to a black bird. Obviously, this message was placed here for your father, and your grandfather felt that he would understand the symbol right away.

Novikov and Sloven had followed Josh to San Francisco. They had parked outside the compound where he was staying with Sarah. They had parked outside the temple where they had gone to services. They were very depressed because of the way things were progressing.

"Things are not going well. We have learned nothing about what Ross was involved in. We are wasting our time and to be honest I am quite bored," said Sloven.

"You are forgetting our orders. We are to follow and observe. Is that too difficult to understand?" replied Novikov.

"Orders, orders, are you brainwashed? We follow and observe nothing in over two months. Contact Dzerzhinsky and tell him we are at a dead end. This Ross fellow has done nothing suspicious other than screw that Israeli brunette. He is a low level bureaucrat, like I told you in Istanbul when he first arrived. The old teacher is dead and so is this mission as far as I am concerned."

CHAPTER 27

Josh and Sarah returned to Monterey. The weather was starting to turn and they encountered quite a bit of coastal fog on the way home.

Sarah settled in as she planned to stay until they had deciphered the message from the tallit bag. She relished the extra time she would be able to spend with Josh, even though he would be busy teaching. At least they would have the whole evenings together.

Sarah studied the message. She had seen this style code before. It was almost an antique as far as codes went. She felt that it would not be difficult to decipher once they had the key document. It was called an Ottendorf Cipher and was common back in the 17th century.

When Josh came home after his class, she told him about the code. He was quite intrigued.

"Sit down and make yourself comfortable. I want you to concentrate," she said.

She grabbed a piece of paper and wrote, "Before we start, let's put on some loud music. If this place is bugged, it will mask our discussion."

Josh nodded in agreement.

As the music played, Sarah continued. "I want you to think back to any specific story your father may have told you at least several times on a regular basis. Even a bedtime story or just idle conversation. I think this might trigger your memory to what we are looking for."

"My father was a great storyteller. He told me many stories of his boyhood days in Russia. Nothing, however, involved a bird of any kind. Wait a minute; he had a favorite poem. It was by that writer who wrote the "Pit and the Pendulum".

"That was Edgar Allen Poe. He wrote the poem "The Raven".

"That was a black bird. Dad recited that many times. He knew it by heart. It was a favorite of his father's. He said he would read it to him when he was little. I'll have to get a copy of the poem in Russian. Maybe it's available at the Military Language School. I'll contact them first thing in the morning and if they have it, we'll see about translating into English and comparing it to the English version. I hope it isn't a problem."

Josh was in luck. He spoke to one of the Russian translators at the Language School who told him that the poem was quite famous in Russia and that there were good translations.

He returned home after obtaining what he needed. That evening they again sat down to tackle the problem.

"There are several ways the Ottendorf Cipher can work," Sarah explained. "Usually the first number refers to the page of the document, then the line and then the letter. We can try that for starters and see what we come up with. Since the "Raven" is a poem, maybe the first number refers to the line in the poem and the next numbers are the letters in the word."

"I knew there was a reason I've been keeping you around, Sarah. You are smarter than I am. What did they teach in Israeli intelligence?"

"I could tell you, Josh, but then I would have to kill you."

"I've heard that one before."

They looked at the message and read off the first line of numbers. It read; 1-11-2. They read the first line of the poem. "Once upon a midnight dreary, while I pondered weak and weary."

"It appears that there is a two letter word on the first line," said Sarah.

"Right you are."

They counted in to the eleventh letter, an 'I'.

The next number was a 2. That was the letter 'N'.

"Put those together and you have the word 'IN'."

"Way to go," said Sarah. "This is fun. Let's do the next line, which is three."

They continued on for several hours, following the same format. There were twenty-six rows of numbers and ninety-nine numbers in all.

A message began to appear as if painted by a master painter:

In the city in the East

Head Man holds a secret

Say thus.

"A man is judged by his deeds not his words"

There it was before them, the whole message. They had done it, and without the help of the U.S. Navy.

They looked at each other, then gave each other a big, congratulatory hug.

The East had to refer to one of the cities his grandfather had been in; Harbin and Mukden. They mulled over what André had related to them in his narrative. With Sarah's almost photographic memory, it did not take them very long to zero in on possible locations.

André had said that the Field Marshal had made his headquarters in one of the homes built by the wealthy Russians who settled in Harbin. The message spoke of a Head Man. There would be no such person in the headquarters except his grandfather.

Outside, up the street and out of sight, Sloven and Novikov kept their watch.

"What do you suppose he was doing at the Language School in such a big hurry?" said Sloven.

"This is the first unusual movement he has made. Everything he has been doing has been routine until now," said Novikov.

"What about the period we lost track of him?" replied Sloven.

"You are right, comrade. He could have been involved with something important, but we will never know, will we.

Tomorrow, we should pay a visit to the school and see if we can find out who he spoke with. Then we can question that person and see if there is anything worth knowing," said Novikov.

"If it wasn't in Harbin, then it has to be Mukden.

Somewhere in Mukden he put this all together and hid the necklace. Think, Sarah, what did André say about what my grandfather did in Mukden?"

"Well, he went there to talk with General Kuropatkin. Afterwards, he went to a very old Buddhist monastery being used as a field hospital and he spent a full day there. André said that the Red Cross was caring for the wounded there in a great way."

"I have a great idea," said Josh. "I'm going to contact the Red Cross and see if they have any historical records on the Russo-Japanese War and their services in Mukden. Perhaps they can tell me which monastery they worked at."

I'm for calling it a night, Sarah. How about you?"

"What did you have in mind, Sweetheart? Let me guess."

The two Russians went to the Language School the following day. With their diplomatic passports they were able to get into the school and speak to the Russian interpreters. Posing a cultural interest, they encountered the interpreter who had spoken to Josh and invited him out for coffee.

It did not take long to get to the subject of his conversation with Josh. The man balked at telling them anything. Novikov told him that if he did not cooperate with them, his family in Russia would suffer the consequences. It just so happened that he did have a brother living in Moscow who was a teacher at the University. He told them exactly what Josh had asked for, a copy of the "Raven" and its Russian English translation. He did not know any more than that.

After they left, the interpreter called Josh at the Graduate School and told him of the encounter.

That evening, Josh retold the story to Sarah.

"Well, they've finally surfaced. I felt like we were being watched, but now we know for certain. Be on your guard, Sarah. We probably can't bring any charges against them. We would not want to endanger the interpreter's brother. On the other hand, if we did, they would claim diplomatic immunity. Let's just play along and see what they do."

The idea of contacting the Red Cross was a good one. They had a historian who had records going back quite some time. They showed that the Red Cross had assisted during the war in 1905. They had the field hospital listed as the "Shenyang Tibetan Monastery", one of the oldest in the city.

"We're finally making some progress," Josh told Sarah. "We know what we're looking for and where it probably is located."

"The message speaks of the head man. That would probably be the head monk. Sixty-three years is a long time and the headman my grandfather spoke to is probably dead and gone. His successor should have been briefed when the title was passed from one monk to another."

"I am sure you are right. The question is how do we get into China?" replied Sarah.

"The secret has been kept these many years. It will keep a little longer until we can find a solution."

CHAPTER 28

Sarah and Josh sat down on the sofa to discuss their relationship. He went to the stereo and turned up the volume on the music.

"I love you, Sarah and I know that you love me. Our lives are not too different. I know you work for Mossad, but there does not have to be a conflict. You know that I believe in the present and future preservation of Israel and all that it stands for."

"I do love you, Josh, and I have come to realize your emotional and political feelings for Israel. I see no conflict whatsoever."

"With that said, I have something I want to give you, something with all my heart."

Josh removed a small velvet box from his pocket and opened it to give to Sarah. The two-carat diamond glittered in anticipation of its new owner.

"Oh my gosh, it's beautiful; yes, yes, of course."

Sarah threw her arms around Josh and gave him an overwhelming kiss.

"You have made me the happiest guy in the whole world, Sarah. I love you more than words can say."

"I know that you are not only here to raise interest and funds to support the immigration of Jews from Russia. I know that André did a lot for Israel and your superiors would like to know what his death was all about. I have thought long and hard about his death. I do not believe he was intentionally murdered. What would they have gained?

"Their objective must have been to find out what he was talking to me about. Killing him accomplished nothing. I believe that they wanted to send a message to him. Stop talking with me was their objective. I think they meant to scare him and they screwed up. They know nothing about our conversations."

"I agree with you, Josh. My dilemma is that I have to keep my superiors appraised of the situation."

"I have no problem with that, Sarah. Tell them we have no specific proof that André was murdered. Tell them the truth: that I believe it was a threat gone bad. At this point in our hunt, we have no definite proof that our treasure is a Russian heirloom. We are not even certain it is, or ever was, where we think it is.

I would like to keep this information our secret, Sarah. I promise you, though, if and when this all comes to fruition I will not object to you telling your superiors that I've been successful in recovering a valuable item entrusted to my grandfather for safekeeping."

"Once you find it, Josh, what are your plans?"

"Once I have it in my possession, it will be my responsibility to safeguard it and carry out the original purpose of the "Present".

"And that would be?"

"If I recall correctly, it was to help save the Russian people. The Russian people are made up of a lot of different people. The Jewish people are one of them.

What if the necklace could be used as a bargaining chip to sway the Russians to let the Jews immigrate to Israel?"

"Josh, if you would do that, it would be fantastic," said Sarah.

"I never thought you were going to keep the necklace for your own personal gain. Personally, I wasn't sure what you wanted to do. I knew that you did not necessarily want to enrich the Soviet Union, I am thrilled with your idea of using the necklace to help save Jewish Russians from a life of persecution and misery, when they could be living in Israel. I will prepare an ample report of my progress thus far. I will say there could be more to it and that I want to pursue it in conjunction with my other objective of raising interest and funds for Jewish emigration.

"So it is agreed; no mention of the necklace to your superiors and I have no reason to tell my government about it, either. At this point, it is all conjecture, anyway.

I have a few more months of teaching here and you have your work. See if you can arrange to stay in the U.S. doing what you have been doing. I'm not sure how long engagements are supposed to last. This is all very new to me."

"Josh, for now we are officially engaged, and that is more than I ever hoped for. I have a very small family left in Israel; my father is a professor of archaeology at the University. My mother passed away some years ago. I have a few cousins. I would love to be married in Israel but I also want to bring our little adventure to a conclusion."

"Anything that will make you happy, Sarah. I have no idea what my next assignment will be but I know that we can both do our best to be together as much as possible."

In the midst of everything, tensions between Israel and her Arab neighbors, which had been building for a long time, finally exploded into warfare. Israel took the initiative and, in one operation, the Israeli Air Forces eliminated the air forces of Egypt, Jordan and Syria. Her army moved into the Sinai and destroyed all Egyptian forces. Israel then moved on the West Bank and Jerusalem and liberated both. Turning then towards Syria, Israel conquered the Golan Heights. All in all, it was a very busy week.

Sarah and Josh were glued to the news, following the army's advances day by day. Sarah wanted so much to be a part of the action, but it was over just as it appeared to be getting started.

Sarah did her part and returned to her fund raising activities. She traveled to Washington and New York and back again to Los Angeles. She did her work with a new enthusiasm, knowing what the greater possibilities might be.

Josh finished teaching his course and was lauded for its uniqueness and beneficial contribution to helping form a more rounded naval officer.

He was surprised at the class commencement exercises when his friend Gabe appeared unannounced.

"When did you arrive, Gabe?"

"Early this morning," he replied. "I'm finished in Turkey. Did you know that the Turks kicked every Greek out of the country?

"So, what brings you here today?"

"I am very close to retiring. The powers that be have asked me to do one last thing. It looks like Nixon is going to be our next president. The word is that he feels it is time to bury the hatchet with China. It is even possible that, sometime during his term, he may engineer a state visit to China. But that is all speculation at this point. I have been asked, as a low level bureaucrat, to initiate some very low level cultural contacts with the Chinese, possibly even talking about starting some trade talks. I want you with me on this, Josh. The Jewish people have had a presence in China for over two thousand years. They have had quite a presence in the East, especially in Harbin. The Chinese are talking about creating a museum there commemorating the good relations between China and the Jews. I think that you could contribute to that.

"Dean Rusk personally asked me to head this up. I mentioned your name and he was quite familiar with your record. He thought you would be a good choice since we are both out of the limelight. What do you think?"

Josh could not believe what he had just heard. He had been racking his brain trying to figure out how he might get into China. Here it was being dropped right into his lap. Fortune was smiling upon him.

"Gabe, the only thing I can say is a one hundred percent yes. I would love to go with you. It will be like old times. I thought we worked together real well, back during the Suez crisis. Before I forget, I have sine great news to tell you. Sarah and I are engaged. No wedding date set yet, but I hope that you and Mary will be able to come to the wedding."

"Congratulations, Josh. I thought you had some interest in André's assistant. You have made a great choice. From what you have told me, and what I already know about her, she is an extremely competent and able woman. I know you both will be very happy."

"I will start the ball rolling to get us to China. I know it will not be easy. The Korean War is still fresh in the minds of many of the leaders. I think the trick, though, is the promise of new trade. China must put their people to work and they do want to raise their standard of living."

Novikov and Sloven were recalled to Moscow as they thought they would be. Dzerzhinsky was not pleased with the outcome of this episode. His agents had learned very little, if anything, about the relationship between the old school teacher and Josh. He had expended an exorbitant amount of money and lost one asset as a result of the auto accident. He must now go to plan B if he was to get to the bottom of this matter. He decided to track Josh's movements through diplomatic channels since he had heard that his teaching assignment in Monterey had been terminated. He was prepared to dispatch two agents immediately if anything viable developed.

When Sarah received the news from Josh about China, she was thrilled. This is what they had been hoping for. She had wangled a possible spot with a group of Jews going to China to discuss the establishment of the new museum being planned in Harbin. It was not definite, but now she would make every effort to go with this group.

CHAPTER 29

Josh returned to Washington, as did Sarah. They both had accomplished a lot over the past year. Josh stayed with a friend, as he was not certain when he would be leaving for the Far East. Sarah stayed at the Israeli Embassy. Her connections seemed unlimited. They were able to spend almost every evening together and every weekend. Their love grew stronger day by day.

After almost forty years in the diplomatic corps, Gabe was very accomplished in the art of diplomacy. Much to his surprise, the Chinese were more than willing to open dialogue with a low level tone, but insisted on keeping it on a secret basis. Saving face was paramount to these people. They did not want to be seen as the ones giving an inch to anyone.

"Josh, I think that we are almost there. To keep us out of the spotlight, the Chinese want to meet in Harbin. It is centrally located for commerce and communications between North and South Asia as well as Europe and the Pacific nations. It is a city rich in culture and Russian influence from the past. Foreign tourists love the city as it is considered the Moscow of the East."

"Gabe, I told you that my grandfather had served there during the Russo-Japanese War. I had hoped that I might visit this area at some time in the future. It looks like the future is now. If you can wangle it, I would like permission to go to Shenyang also, it is a major political, economic and cultural center to the South. Tell them that the close proximity of these two cities to Pacific ports makes them ideal areas for us to focus on when and if trade actually begins once again."

"Excellent point," replied Gabe. "I will do my best."

"Point of information," said Josh. "Sarah might be traveling to Harbin with a Jewish committee looking into the establishment of a Jewish museum. Is that a problem?"

"You two are not cooking up something are you?"

"Now, Gabe, what makes you say that? You know I have always been on the up and up with you."

"I sense there is something you are not telling me. Is there?"

"I told you that my grandfather served and died in this area. I never met the man. The things I learned in Istanbul have been nagging at my brain for a long time. I want to learn all I can about him and his exploits. If I can actually stand where he stood, it would be extraordinary."

"I can feel your need, Josh," replied Gabe.

"Like I said, I will do my best to make it happen."

CHAPTER 30

With all the new developments, Josh and Sarah decided to meet and make some tentative plans. Sarah invited Josh to the embassy, as she wanted to show him off anyway to her colleagues.

"Sarah, you look radiant."

"Why shouldn't I? You make me shine so much. It is not every day that an Israeli has a U.S. diplomat as a fiancé."

They sat in Sarah's small suite and discussed the recent developments. It was decided that if Sarah made it to Harbin, she would try and get permission to go to Shenyang also. She would then check out the Shenyang Tibetan Monastery. Hopefully, it would still be open and the monks accessible to talk with. Returning to

Harbin, she would brief Josh and he could then act on her information.

"Josh, if we pull this off, it will be a miracle. I never thought we would get this far. We are so close and yet so far. The message from your grandfather seems like a fairy tale. If I ever told anyone, I doubt if they would believe me."

"Well, don't tell anyone. Not yet anyway. Not until I have the necklace safely in my hands and I am out of China."

"What will you do with it once you get it?"

"I am working on that. For starters, I will put it in a bank vault in Zurich where I know it will be safe."

Having made their plans, Sarah and Josh parted once again. Josh learned that he would be leaving for the Far East very shortly with Gabe. Arrangements had been made and marching orders issued. They were called to the State Department and given the blessing of the Secretary, personally.

The Soviet Embassy had been alerted when Josh appeared on the scene in Washington. Dzerzhinsky wanted Ross tracked, to say the least. When the Soviets followed Josh and Gabe to the airport and found out that they had a flight to Hong Kong, they immediately contacted Dzerzhinsky and asked for instructions. He said he would handle it from Moscow.

Novikov and Sloven were dispatched to the Soviet Embassy in Beijing. They awaited instructions from the Hong Kong Agent in Charge as to the ultimate destinations of the two diplomats.

Josh and Gabe had a good flight. It was very long but the service on the big Pan Am jet was outstanding. They always felt like they were back in the U.S. of A when they flew on Pan Am. The airline had such a presence all over the world; many people believed that it belonged to the U.S. Government.

They were met by Chinese representatives in Hong Kong and whisked away to a good hotel in the city. They were told that they would be flown by private plane to Harbin, to stay under the diplomatic radar.

The meetings in Harbin were very cool for starters. Josh and Gabe worked hard to present the sincere desire of the United Sates to look to the future and not the past. Germany had been an enemy and was now an ally. Japan had been an enemy and was now an ally. The United

States hoped that China would at least enter into an era of reconciliation and mutual respect. The sincerity of the two men was the catalyst in warming the Chinese.

Sarah arrived not too long after the two diplomats. Their hosts welcomed her small group warmly. Sarah and her small entourage were shown the proposed old synagogue that the Chinese wanted to turn into a museum commemorating the thousand years of Jewish history in this area of China.

Many ideas were presented on both sides and it was agreed they would meet again at a future date after all the recommendations had been thoroughly investigated.

Sarah asked for special permission to travel to Shenyang located about a day's ride to the south. Permission was granted with a young female political escort.

The city of Shenyang teemed with people. Commerce seemed to be thriving everywhere. Sarah expressed her interest in old Buddhist temples and other ancient cultures of the Chinese. Her escort happily showed her around the city and they had an opportunity to venture into some of the oldest monasteries.

At the Shenyang monastery she lingered; looking at all the delicate architecture and attempting to speak with the monks. To her dismay, the head monk was not present. He was away on a pilgrimage to visit the Dalai Lama in Dharamshala. She obtained the monk's name and thanked the tour escort for his patience.

The return trip to Harbin was uneventful and Sarah, once again, thanked her Chinese host for his kindness.

Josh was just completing his round of talks with the other members of the meeting. He mentioned his interest in the museum that was under consideration. His hosts were more than happy to show him the proposed building.

To his good fortune, he was introduced to the delegation of Jews and, of course, Sarah.

She had no way of knowing where Josh had been holding his meetings as it was considered top secret, to say the least.

"Josh, it is so wonderful to see you," she whispered.

"I made it to Shenyang and found the monastery. I even got the name of the head monk. Unfortunately, he was away, visiting the Dalai Lama in India. What are you going to do now?"

"We are too close to accept defeat. I am going to try to go to Dharamshala and meet with the monk. What was his name?"

"Jot this down; Tenzin Paljor."

"Sarah, we have no time to lose. I don't know how those two Russians found out we were in China. But, I'm sure that I saw someone who looked like Sloven hanging around our hotel. I'll tell Gabe that I would like to meet the Dalai Lama. I am going to take some personal time and go to India. I can work it into my return trip to the U.S.

"I would love to go with you. Do you think it is possible?"

"Why not?"

CHAPTER 31

Within the week, Sarah and Josh were on their way. Sloven and Novikov were right on their tail. They had not known of Sarah's trip to Shenyang and they only knew of Josh's presence in the city.

Josh and Sarah arrived in New Delhi and made connections to Dharamsala. It was a difficult trip, but once in Dharamsala, it was well worth the effort. The city was a beehive of activity. There was a major festival in progress, with many more to come. The mountains in the distance above the valley were some of the most beautiful they had ever seen. The valley, called Kangra, was very fertile. They saw wheat and rice growing in great abundance. The streets were filled with tourists, both young and old.

Josh wasted no time in applying for an audience with the Dalai Lama. He mentioned the monk from Shenyang, hoping it would improve his chances. The trick worked and within the week they were walking past the great Central Cathedral to the residence of His Holiness.

They met with the personal secretary of His Holiness and were told the Dalai Lama would meet with them within the hour. The meeting was extraordinary. His Holiness was so welcoming and polite in every respect.

"Mr. Ross, your name is not unknown to me. If I recall correctly, you were one of the individuals who helped bring about peace in the Suez War of 1956," said the Dalai Lama.

"That is correct. I was there but played a small part in the negotiations."

"You are too modest. Miss Burstein, I understand that you are attempting to raise funds for the Refuseniks in the Soviet Union. Our work is very similar. I, too, am attempting to free my people from their oppressive life in China. I have been gone almost ten years and their lot has only grown worse."

"Your Holiness," said Josh. "Many years ago my grandfather met one of your monks. The year was 1905. In that it was so long ago, I doubt whether he is still with us. The monastery was in Shenyang and the monks had allowed the monastery to be used as a hospital for Russian soldiers. I understand that the current headman, Tenzin Paljor, is here in Dharamsala on a pilgrimage. Would it be possible for me to meet with him and discuss a personal matter relating to my grandfather?"

"If he is still here, I will be most happy to direct him to you. If there is nothing else, it has been my pleasure to meet with you both and I wish you peace and tranquility in your lives."

His Holiness, the Dalai Lama, rose from his chair and left the room. The personal secretary approached and directed them to a smaller anteroom close by. It was not more than 15 minutes later when an old monk entered the room and bowed slightly to the couple.

"I am Tenzin Paljor, head man at Shenyang. How can I be of service to you?"

"It is an honor to meet you. May I be so personal as to ask how long you have been head monk at Shenyang?"

"A long time, Sir. I rose to this position almost fifty years ago. I will be ninety-five years old next week and I will retire soon to tend my flowers."

"Many years ago, in 1905, before you were head man, my grandfather visited your monastery when it was being used as a field hospital for Russian troops. He toured your monastery and spoke extensively with the head man."

"That would have been Sonam, my predecessor."

Josh looked straight into Tenzin's eyes and, very slowly and clearly said,

"A man is judged by his deeds, not his words."

Tenzin stared at Josh for a long moment and then a small smile formed on his face.

"You are the one I was told who might come one day. I was given specific instructions regarding your coming. I had actually put it out of my mind; it was so long ago. I remember your grandfather passing out medals to the wounded soldiers. Such a small reward for such a big sacrifice."

"To tell you the truth, Sir, other than my grandfather's quote, I have no idea what this all means."

"Your grandfather left something with us for safekeeping. He feared he might die in battle and he did not want the package to be lost. It is in a safe place within the monastery. I will be returning to Shenyang in several weeks. You are most welcome to meet me there on my return."

"I work for the United States Department of State. I hope that I can return to your country soon. You know the situation, I am sure. I wish you a very happy birthday and good health. Thank you for this meeting and I will make every attempt to see you in the near future."

With that, Josh and Sarah said goodbye and left the residence.

In a small café not far from the residence, Novikov and Sloven sat reading a newspaper and drinking tea.

"What do you suppose that was all about?"

"I have told you before, Novikov, we are wasting our time. They are tourists like all the others; everyone who comes to Dharamsala wants to meet the Dalai Lama. He has become a rock star more famous than Elvis Presley."

"Sloven, if you ever hope to advance
in this business you have to realize that
watching and waiting to catch the rabbit
eventually leads to rabbit stew for dinner.
We have been following this Ross fellow for
a long time. Do I know any more than I did
when we started? Not really.

Do I suspect that there is more to
know? Yes. And I will tell you why; because
Dzerzhinsky says so. I listen to what that
man says. "

CHAPTER 32

Josh and Sarah returned to Washington. They both felt they had accomplished a lot. Their trip to Dharamsala had been more than they expected. They did not know when they would return to China. They hoped it would be before Tenzin Paljor passed to the next world. He had looked pretty good for ninety-five and he did not seem to have a lot of stress in his life. But you never knew.

"Josh, what shall I tell my superiors about our activities? I have to tell them something, especially since the Russians seem to be following our every move."

"What to tell them? Tell them I may have found some unique leverage to help Israel convince the U.S.S.R. to let a lot of Jews immigrate to Israel. Do not say any more than that. Just say I am not telling you any more than that."

"Josh, you amaze me. You could sweet talk anyone."

"I just do not want to jump the gun; keep them hanging. They have nothing to lose and everything to gain."

Josh went to see his superiors. They were pleased with what had transpired in Harbin. Nixon would surely begin to implement new policies that he thought best for the country. The rumor was that China was high on his priority list. He wanted change, real change. It was even rumored that a State visit was on the table.

Josh and Gabe were debriefed in great detail about the tone of the meetings in Harbin. No one likes to be rejected, including the President of the United States. Once he made an offer, he wanted it to be accepted.

Their opinions were accepted warmly and it was decided that when and if, negotiations started in earnest, Josh would be a key player. They liked his style, and most of all, he got results. Josh began the preliminary tasks of planning the next meeting and what would be discussed.

He and Sarah decided they would lease a small apartment, since it appeared that they would be in Washington awhile.

Novikov and Sloven, much to their liking, had also been posted to Washington to continue their task of watching and waiting. Novikov was certain that something had to break soon.

Despite all the effort of many people both in Israel and the United States, the Refusniks in the Soviet Union were being denied exit visas over and over. Teachers, scientists, doctors, and people from all walks of life, wanted to leave. The Soviets were relentless in their refusals.

After all this time, Dzerzhinsky was becoming impatient. He decided to go to plan B. He contacted Novikov and Sloven and gave them their marching orders.

The following, evening after dinner, Sarah told Josh that she had been called to an unexpected meeting at the Israeli Embassy. She kissed him goodbye and told him not to wait up for her, as she would be late.

Leaving their apartment in Georgetown, a decent neighborhood, Sarah had no reason to suspect that she would be in any danger from the criminal element. As she walked towards the bus stop, a man approached from the opposite direction. It was getting dark and she could not see his face. As he got closer she recognized him; it was Novikov, and he was smiling.

Sarah quickly was on her guard. She had been trained well in Israel and she was not afraid to use her skills. Her focus was riveted on the approaching target. That was her undoing. Unseen by her, Sloven slipped up from behind and in one quick, expert motion, covered her face with a chloroform mask. Within seconds, a blue van pulled to the curb. A hood was thrown over her head and she was thrown into the van like a sack of potatoes.

The van proceeded towards the Soviet Embassy. It stopped short of it and pulled into a parking garage. Once inside, it was driven all the way to the rear and aboard a freight elevator. Traveling downward for at least thirty seconds, the elevator stopped and the van exited. The two spies removed Sarah from the vehicle and opened an electronic door. Once inside, they took Sarah to one of the several rooms within the suite.

The men placed masks over their own faces and removed her hood. They placed her in a chair, securely tying her feet and arms behind her.

A new character in a mask approached her and placed some smelling salts under her nose to revive her. She coughed several times and attempted to vomit her supper, but nothing came.

Sloven approached her. "My dear, Miss Burstein, You realize that you are in a real predicament. There is no one who can help you except yourself. It is very easy. We will ask you a few questions and we expect truthful answers. If you answer all of our questions we will let you go unharmed, back to the arms of your boyfriend."

Sarah had been trained for such an unpleasant event, but being just a little headstrong she was not about to cooperate with these common thugs who had been annoying, bumbling fools since Istanbul. She chided herself for allowing herself to be grabbed by these amateurs. She decided to see how far they intended to go before she fed them a story.

"First question; what is your name and nationality?"

"You already know my name and that I am an Israeli, unless you are a totally incompetent fool who should be catching dogs on the streets of Moscow."

"Wrong answer," said Sloven, as he hauled off and smacked her face hard enough to bring tears to her eyes and make her ears ring.

"Do you admit that you are an Israeli agent?"

"I am an Israeli here in the United States to raise money to help Soviet Jews who are tired of eating Russian borscht and stale bread."

"Wrong again," and he doubled his fist and hit her in her chest, totally knocking the wind out of her.

"I have no other appointments tonight, Miss Burstein. I can keep this up all night until I hear what I want and you keep your Jew humor to yourself."

The last hit had really startled Sarah. This lug was really strong. She composed herself after several minutes of silence and said,

"What else do you want to know besides my being an Israeli fund raiser and my name, which you seem to have got down pat?"

"Your humor is not helping you. I'm warning you."

"I have no idea why you have made me a target. I really know very little. I have worked as a secretary at a college for an old man you murdered. I now work as a fundraiser, as I told you, and, as you know, I am dating a diplomat of the United Sates. My life is not complex. I am a kibbutz girl who made it to the city, nothing more.

"Do you take us for fools?" asked Novikov.

"Do you really want me to answer that question," replied Sarah.

Once again, Sloven took the palms of his hands and smashed them simultaneously against Sarah's eardrums.

The pressure was unbearable and she thought that her eardrums had been blown away. It took her over five minutes to regain any composure.

"Are you an agent of Mossad?"

"I work for Mossad as a secretary, nothing more."

"We do not believe you. Time to advance you to higher education," replied Novikov.

"This next course is graduate level so I would think long and hard before you answer."

"Are you an agent of Mossad?"

"I wanted to be a cryptographer for them but they said I was not smart enough. They did say that I did very good secretarial work for them."

"Miss Burstein, you have been selected for the graduate level education."

Ivan who had been leaning up against the wall, wheeled over a high amp, battery charger from the corner. He took two of the charger's long cables and attached one to each of Sarah's ears. He then rubbed each one and smiled broadly, in anticipation of what was to come.

"Are you an agent of Mossad?"

Sarah did not answer. She braced herself for what she knew would be a terrific shock. She had experienced this before in training and it always had been very unpleasant. She knew that they wanted information and would not kill her before getting it.

Nevertheless, the shock was bone jarring. They did not start out with a low charge. They were tiring of her attitude and her answers. She was almost rendered unconscious. A bucketful of ice-cold water splashed over her, reviving her somewhat.

"Let us not push too hard or too fast, comrade," said Novikov.

He slapped her face lightly, several times, to get attention.

"Miss Burstein, we do not want to hurt you."

"Sure, sure, I trust you implicitly."

"What is your relationship with Ross?"

"We are engaged to be married, if I make it out of here alive."

"What did Ross want with the Turkish teacher?"

"He had him translate a letter he had received from a cousin in Russia."

"Nothing more?" asked Novikov.

"Nothing more, I promise," she said as she let several tears run down her face.

"Here, here, Miss Burstein, do not cry. See how easy this is when you answer the questions honestly."

"What is Ross' relationship with Naval Intelligence? And do not lie to us."

"He taught a course in diplomacy, nothing more."

Sarah started to nod off. Novikov told Ivan to put the amps on low and give her a jolt.

The shock woke Sarah up quickly and she glared at Novikov.

"How much longer are you going to ask me questions that you already know the answers to?"

"What business did you have in Harbin, China?

"Answer me truthfully or so help me, I will have Ivan turn the amps on full.

"No, please, no," cried Sarah. "I was invited by the Chinese to assist in the plans for a new Jewish museum; nothing more."

"What was Ross doing there?"

"He could not tell me, something secret he said. The Chinese had invited him. You're friendly with the Chinese, ask them."

"Be careful, I still have your ears wired and I will make your hair stand straight up if I feel you are lying to me."

"Please, no more. I have told you the truth, every bit of it."

"What was the purpose of your visit with the Dalai Lama?"

"Mr. Ross always wanted to meet the Dalai Lama.

We decided to stop off and see Dharamsala on the way home, nothing more. We were just tourists, like so many others there. That is the truth. I can't take any more of your higher education, please believe me. I have told you the truth."

Novikov and Sloven conversed quietly in the corner of the room.

"I told you, Novikov, we are wasting our time. She knows nothing. You have beaten her up and burned her ears. She has told you nothing except information you could put in a travel brochure."

"I don't know," said Novikov. "My gut feeling is that she is giving us a snow job worse than the Siberian winters. I feel like one more big jolt of juice and see what her answer will be."

"Ok," said Sloven. "One more jolt and let's pack up and get out of here. She has ruined my whole evening. Let's drug her and throw her off in the street near where we picked her up. They will think she got molested by one of those D.C. weirdoes and let it go at that."

Once more, they turned the amps on to one hundred percent and held the switch for a good ten seconds. Sarah blacked out as her ears began to smoke.

They revived her once more with smelling salts and ice water. She began to shake and shiver.

"Last question, Miss Burstein, and it will be the last question you ever answer if you do not tell us the truth," said Novikov.

"Are you and Ross engaged in any activities that will endanger the Union of the Soviet Socialist Republic? Think about your answer or I will burn you to a crisp just like at Auschwitz."

"No, No," moaned Sarah. "I have told you the truth; I promise, nothing bad, I am a good girl. I would not hurt anyone or anything."

"She is starting to get delirious. I don't think we are going to get anything else from her," said Sloven.

They chloroformed Sarah one more time and placed the hood over her head. They untied her from the chair. Once more they threw her in the van and returned to the place where they had grabbed her. They untied her hands and feet. After making sure no one was in the area, or looking from a nearby window, they tossed her from the van.

Sarah was beside herself. She thought they would surely slit her throat and she would be another D.C. murder case. She removed the hood and could not believe she was only a block from her apartment.

She slowly regained her composure as she sat on the curb. She was thankful to be alive.

Those bastards are dead meat if I am ever given the chance. I will not think twice. If I have a knife, I will slit their throats. If I have my gun, I will empty the clip. They are dead meat.

She rose from the curb and dragged herself the full block to her apartment. She banged on the door until Josh came running out.

CHAPTER 33

Surprisingly, Sarah did not cry as Josh cradled her in his arms and carried her to the bedroom. She slowly related the evening's events, reassuring Josh that she divulged nothing to the goons who had grabbed her, except things they probably already knew. She did tell him that she thought that they would kill her if they did not burn her to death.

Josh was furious. He was prepared to call a black ops friend of his and have Novikov and Sloven whacked.

"Don't," said Sarah. "I have plans for these guys, if I ever have the chance. They are dead meat. When I get through with them, their own mother will not recognize them."

With that, she collapsed on the bed and fell fast asleep.

It took several weeks of rest and medical care for Sarah to return to normal. Josh even forced her to see a psychologist to insure there was no lingering mental trauma. Sarah was extremely strong, both physically and mentally. Her life in Israel had been built on hardship as a child. Forced marches through the mountains as a child to escape the Arab attacks on her kibbutz were forever imbedded in her memory. Her tour in the army, and then being solicited to join Mossad, had hardened her to cope with no matter what obstacles or hardship she might ever face.

Josh and Gabe spent countless hours discussing the results of the meetings with the Chinese. Their objective was clearly in sight but the correct path to arriving at it was debated endlessly by selected experts who knew the Chinese psyche better than anyone. America's new president wanted good results above everything. He hoped his legacy would be an end to China as a threat and the formulation of a world class-trading partner whose markets would absorb an endless supply of U.S. made goods.

Gabe asked for an extension on his upcoming retirement so he could see this project through to fruition. The State Department saw him and Josh as a varsity team with a winning record. Gabe would stay on.

The time finally came for a return visit to Harbin, and the Chinese. Josh and Gabe were ready. If things went well, it could pave the way for President Nixon's proposed plans in the coming future.

Sarah was elated for Josh. She knew this would be their best chance to get to the monastery and Tenzin Paljor. Her discussions with her superiors on Josh's potential leverage with the Soviets for new immigration were enough to want her to concentrate all her efforts on helping him. Sarah would return to Harbin with the guise of a follow up on the Jewish museum.

CHAPTER 34

Novikov and Sloven did not need a special invitation.

They received their clearances from their Embassy and were once again airborne to China to monitor their charges.

The new meetings with the Chinese were interminable. It could be likened to a poker game between master players, each one raising and calling the other to win the game. But in the end, and after countless days, a semblance of a meeting of minds had been agreed to.

Josh and Gabe took a much-needed breather. Gabe decided on a trip to Hong Kong and Josh on an extended visit to Shenyang.

Sarah had been spending her time meeting with the various cultural delegations going over the plans for the proposed museum. She assured them that she could be influential in securing additional funds from other Jewish agencies to assist in the construction.

Josh and Sarah then sat down to formulate their plan.

"We must keep an extremely low profile if we are to get to Shenyang and then out of China in one piece. I am going to presume we are not without our bird dogs. Once we have what we came for, I want to get to Credit Suisse in Zurich and put the necklace in a vault."

"Josh, I know that we will have our diplomatic status. But that has not stopped our Soviet friends from doing what they will. I, for one, want to be prepared, if and when I meet those bastards again. Any objections?"

"Like, prepared how?"

"I want to obtain a Walther PPK, my weapon of choice. I am sure we can get one for enough U.S. dollars. Are you against guns?"

"I am quite familiar with guns, Sarah. I would rather use words, but I cannot forget your face when you came back that night. I am all for being prepared. Let's do it, by all means. I'll advise Gabe that we'll return to the U.S. by way of Israel and Switzerland. Once we're out of China, there are a lot of details that must be ironed out in order for our plans to become reality."

"OK, I will contact some of my Jewish friends here and see about a weapon. If you will see about our trip to Shenyang with the authorities, we should be on our way soon."

Novikov and Sloven had no idea why the pair had now gone south to Shenyang. They surmised it could have been another sight-seeing venture, but they had their doubts.

"I know what our orders are, Novikov. Don't you think we should contact Dzerzhinsky for additional instructions?"

"For once you might be right, comrade. I, too, am tiring of this wild goose chase. If nothing comes of this after all this time, then I am all for a little accident to befall our friends."

"Let's propose that to Dzerzhinsky and see what he says."

Sarah and Josh made it to their hotel and decided that the first order of business was a good dinner and a good night's rest. Tomorrow would be one of the biggest days in their lives if all went well.

CHAPTER 35

The Chinese guide assigned to Josh and Sarah drove them into the heart of the city.

"We would like to walk awhile if it is OK with you. We get a much better feel for the people and the beautiful architecture," said Josh. "Point us in the direction of the old Buddhist monastery of Shenyang. We have heard so much about it."

"A wise choice. It is very historic and has some of the most beautiful Buddhas inside. Also, the gardens, designed by the monks, are well known throughout this region. It is not far from here. You both enjoy your walk, and I will meet you outside the monastery in an hour," stated the guide.

Novikov and Sloven followed close behind. Once again they had their doubts where this would lead but they had their instructions.

Josh and Sarah approached the old monastery. He wondered how his grandfather felt when he had come here. It was being used as a hospital then, and inside were the dying and the dead.

"Do you think Tenzin is still alive?" said Sarah.

"I hope he is well enough to show us around, and give us what he has for us."

They approached the massive wooden doors of the monastery. There did not appear to be anyone around. They knocked, and shortly thereafter, the door to their left opened ever so slightly.

"The monastery is not yet open," said an old monk.

"We have come a long way from Dharamsala to see an old friend, Tenzin Paljor," said Josh.

"Tenzin is not well today. Can you come another day?"

"Our visas expire tomorrow, and today is the only day we have.

"What is your name?"

"Tell Tenzin, A man is judged by his deeds not by his words. He will understand."

With that, the old monk left them and went deep into the monastery. After a while, the monk returned and beckoned them inside. They walked down a long, wide corridor until they arrived at a huge Buddha at the far end. The monk again motioned them to follow and they entered a large room behind the statue.

The walls of the room were covered with beautiful tapestries. A large candelabra with at least a dozen candles lit the room. At the far end was a simple pallet with a thin mattress on which a frail old man sat.

"You have returned," said the old monk. "I am sorry for my ill health. I have lived much longer than I expected. I am thankful for each day, as it is a blessing. I hoped I would live to see you again. What has been entrusted to me has been a burden on my mind. The possession itself has been no trouble. The responsibility of giving it to you has weighed upon me for many years, especially as I have gotten older. I feared for my memory most of all."

"I am certain that my grandfather never intended this to be a burden on you and your order. I think that he was faced with very few options at the time and he chose your monastery and your monks because of the trust he felt when he visited here, so many years ago."

"Your words ring true. I feel I can gather my strength once more today to conclude this responsibility to you and your grandfather."

With that, the old monk rose from his bed, put on his sandals, and shuffled down the room. He led them past the great Buddha and down another corridor. At the far end he descended a steep staircase. Halfway down, he stopped to rest and catch his breath.

"Only a little further, my friends."

The staircase descended another flight that ended at the base of a long corridor.

The monk proceeded down the corridor with Josh and Sarah close behind. This hallway was twice as long as the last one. At the far end stood a smaller Buddha, gilded in gold.

"This is our oldest Buddha, brought here from Tibet. It is several thousands of years old and very precious to us."

Tenzin approached the Buddha and knelt before it in prayer. After several minutes, he rose and circled behind the statue. Josh and Sarah followed close behind.

Once behind the Buddha, Tenzin removed a small, flat key from his robe and inserted it into a small crevice, hardly visible to the naked eye. A clicking sound could be heard as a small panel slid open.

"I must be very careful from here on in. I have never done this before. If I make a mistake, I could lose my hand. These devices were designed thousands of years ago to keep out the unfaithful. I was instructed on how to proceed over fifty years ago. Let me rest a moment and recollect my thoughts."

"Take all the time you need, Tenzin. We have all day," said Josh. "If I can help, just ask."

After a short while, Tenzin inserted his hand into the open space in the Buddha. A series of clicks were again heard and another panel slid open inside the Buddha.

Tenzin withdrew his hand and wiped the sweat upon his robe.

"So far so good," he said.

He again inserted his hand and then removed it, holding a package wrapped in the flag of Imperial Russia.

"This belongs to you, Mr. Ross. I have completed my responsibility. I hope that whatever is within this flag, brings you the satisfaction that was intended. I wish you well on your journey and, above all, I wish you peace of mind that comes with doing the deeds of the heart. I will rest here with Buddha awhile. If you proceed down the hall and ascend the steps, you will find yourselves in the main hall.

"Please accept my heartfelt thanks, Tenzin."

He handed Josh the package neatly covered by the imperial flag and bowed slightly as they departed.

Josh and Sarah walked the long hall to the stairs. There, they stopped and sat on the steps. Josh unwrapped the flag. It was a beautiful thing itself. The flag was red silk with white bands radiating from the corners. In the center was a circle with a crown on top. Inside the circle was the imperial eagle holding lightning bolts in his claws. Above the eagle was a banner with three words in Russian. Josh recognized the first word as God.

He held the package in his hands. It was quite heavy.

He slowly unwrapped the thin layers of muslin that covered it. As he unwrapped the last layer, a ray of light sparkled off the first row of diamonds. Removing the last layer of cloth revealed the most magnificent emeralds, rubies and sapphires they had ever seen.

"Josh, you have it. It is the coronation necklace. I remember the picture from the Smithsonian. It is a wondrous creation. It puts Napoleon's necklace to shame."

Josh stared at the treasure. He ran his fingers over diamonds that were the size of small walnuts. The emeralds were all perfectly matched and were the deepest green he had ever seen. He gave a long sigh and closed his eyes.

"It has taken us so long to arrive at this point, Sarah.

I know in my heart what I want to do. I just hope that the rest of this adventure turns out the way we hope. I would hate to have this treasure fall into the wrong hands."

He carefully wrapped the necklace with the muslin cloth and then wrapped the Tsar's flag around the whole package. He placed it within his leather briefcase and attached a diplomatic seal over the snap lock.

"This should get us through customs and any prying eyes."

They climbed the two flights of stairs; walked the length of the great hall and exited through the massive wood doors. The bright sunlight blinded them at first but the warmth of the sun made them feel good to be alive.

Novikov and Sloven watched the pair as they left the monastery.

"They were in there a long time," said Sloven.

"What do you think happened?"

"I have no way of knowing. We will only find out if we can question them like we did the woman. We will follow them and bide our time."

CHAPTER 36

They left Shenyang the following day, heading for Hong Kong. Once there, they boarded Pan Am for the long flight to Istanbul. They connected with El Al and flew straight to Tel Aviv.

Sarah called her father in Jerusalem and, that evening, they all sat down to dinner in the King David Hotel.

"Sarah has told me so much about you, Josh. You two have been flying around the world. Anything special going on? Sarah is very tight lipped. Never tells me very much about her work."

"I cannot say much, either. Everything is good though, and the future will reveal everything."

"Josh, you sound like an archeologist, like myself. Except, when I dig, I reveal the past."

"I have been very involved in the past. I have not done much digging, but I have done a lot of searching. Sarah has been at my side the whole time and, I must say, she has learned her skills well from someone."

"When will you two be getting married?"

"We have a few loose ends to tie up and then we can sit down and set the date. Of course, you will give Sarah away and we would like to be married in Jerusalem with all the family."

"I am sure that it all can be arranged. You keep me posted of the date and send me the invitations. I will insure that everyone in the family will be there."

The two watchers sat outside the hotel reading the paper. Novikov and Sloven were masters of disguise; beards one day, a longer nose, different color hair the next. Maybe, they thought, we should have gone into the theater, rather than pursuing surveillance, which in this case, seemed pretty unsuccessful so far. How much longer would they have to continue at their posts, they wondered. The long airplane rides were starting to grate on their nerves. The hotels they stayed in were what rubles could afford and that was not much these days.

After dinner and goodbyes, Josh and Sarah retired to their room.

"I want to meet with your superior, Sarah, your number one man in Mossad. Can you arrange it?"

"I'm sure I can; that would be David Bar Simone. That name is classified by the way, so use it very sparingly."

The following day was just beautiful. The sun, bright and the air cool, and Josh felt for a moment that he was back in California. He wondered when he would see home again. These many months had him traveling the globe and he still was not sure when it would all end.

They arrived at Mossad headquarters, a nondescript building like every other newer building in Jerusalem. Sarah showed her credentials and they were ushered into an office on the third floor. A very athletic-looking man with a full crop of silver hair sat at the desk, smoking a pipe.

"Welcome to Israel, Josh Ross. We have been following your travels with great interest. You might say that Sarah Burstein has been our tour guide in your behalf. We hope she has been a good traveling companion. I see by the engagement ring on her finger that things have not gone too badly."

"David Bar Simone, it is a pleasure to meet you. I have willingly asked Sarah to keep you up to date on the particulars of what we have been pursuing. What I am about to divulge to you I would like kept as secret as possible until I can conclude it all."

"It all sounds very secretive already. What is the big secret?"

"Sarah told you of our meeting with André Zommer. He told me things about my family that I was not aware of. My grandfather was a confident of Tsar Nicholas II. He also was close to the Tsarina Alexandra. In 1904, fearing for her life and her family, she entrusted to my grandfather for safekeeping a valuable treasure of the Russian empire. It was given to him with the stipulation that it be used to help the Russian people. Sarah and I have recovered the treasure. It was a long and hard search and discovery process. I have it safely stored in a safe place.

"The Present, as I like to refer to it, is the coronation necklace given by Peter the Great to his wife Catherine upon her coronation. It is a priceless heirloom of the Russian people and I am certain that the Soviet Government would be willing to barter almost anything for its return."

"If it is authentic as you say it is, I believe that you are absolutely right. It would have great bargaining power."

"Let's you and I see if we can start a bargaining process. The Soviets have had several agents shadowing us from the beginning. We believe that they are the ones who murdered Zommer. Their boss is KGB. I am sure you know his name."

"That would be Ivan Dzerzhinsky, current head of the KGB. His grandfather was the founder of the KGB, Felix Dzerzhinsky. His father is Nikolai Dzerzhinsky, former head of the KGB, now retired living in Sochi."

"I would like you to contact Ivan on the QT when I tell you. First, I have some details to take care of in Switzerland at a bank. I want a meeting set up between you, me, Sarah and Ivan in Zurich. I will negotiate with the Soviets as an individual, no mention of the United Sates. I will return the necklace to the Soviets when

100,000 Jews have been allowed to leave the U.S.S.R and have arrived safely in Israel. We will pay all transportation costs. The Soviets will pay for ink and the paper the exit visas are printed on. What do you think?"

"You should set up shop in the bazaar. I honestly don't know if they will buy into that. Sarah, what is your take on all this?"

"The Soviets think the necklace was stolen by the guards of the royal family. It is a priceless treasure. I think they would do anything to get it back. What are 100,000 Jews to them? They sent five times that number to die in Siberia. We hold all the cards. Broach the subject and let's see how the cards play out. We have the royal flush."

They all agreed to talk again once Josh had concluded his arrangements in Zurich.

They left the following day with the full knowledge that the two agents of the Soviets were following them.

"Josh, we have to do something about the Russians. I personally know what I would like to do with them."

"Let's see how this plays out. First, we go to the Credit Suisse in Zurich. I make arrangement with the bank on the possession of the safety deposit box. Once that has been done, we can arrange to meet with Dzerzhinsky here in Zurich. Maybe he will call off his watchdogs then."

CHAPTER 37

Novikov and Sloven had already received new instructions from Moscow; liquidate the man and the woman.

After Josh and Sarah arrived in Zurich, they rented a large, Citroen sedan and decided on a couple of hours of sightseeing before heading to the bank in the afternoon. They drove south towards the city and Lake Zurich. At this time of the day, the road was relatively traffic free.

Once they arrived at the Lake they began to look for a place to have lunch. As Josh slowed down for a curve, Novikov and Sloven reduced the distance between the two vehicles. They had decided to force them off the road, shoot them and then set their car on fire.

Josh spotted the high-speed approach of the other car. Sarah was aware also. She was prepared. Josh deliberately spun his rear wheels into a dirt side road, sending up a terrific cloud of dust, then quickly returned to the paved main road and over to the other lane. Novikov, who was driving, failed to catch that maneuver and, in a few moments, was alongside Josh on the inside. Josh spun his wheel, crashing into the side of Novikov's car. The Russians were forced off the road and well into the dirt and trees.

Josh pulled off the road in front of them, blocking any movement on their part. Sloven was out of the car first. In his hand he held a P6 semi-automatic with a silencer.

Sarah was also well armed with her Walther PPK. She had extra clips in her pocket. She fired three shots into their chests. Sloven went down like a load of bricks. Novikov was out of the car and crouching on the ground. He aimed his Steyr GB automatic and fired two rounds at Sarah. One shot had hit her in the shoulder and forced her to drop her gun. Josh dove for Sarah's gun just as Novikov was taking aim again at Sarah. Sloven screamed for help from his comrade distracting him momentarily. That gave Josh the second he needed. He grabbed

Sarah's gun and fired the rest of the clip into Novikov's head, bursting it like a melon. Sarah was up and crawling over to Josh. She handed him another clip.

"Finish the other one off. This game has no prisoners.

Josh loaded the clip; went over to Sloven and fired seven rounds into his head. There was no doubt about the outcome. They dragged the two bodies to their car; pushed it further into the shrubs; rigged an easy torch to the gas tank and lit the fuse. The car burst into flames, and in less than five minutes, everything in the car was being burnt beyond recognition.

"I do not like to take a life, but when my life is in question I do not hesitate. He who hesitates is lost. They meant to kill us. We were lucky," said Sarah.

"You were great," said Josh. "I have not fired a gun in years. I was very lucky today. My old Colt 45 would have surely stopped him. With your Walther, I had to shoot him in the head to be sure."

"Josh, you were very quick. I didn't see the other one at first. I am glad you were able to take him out. Let's get out of here now. I think the bullet went clean through the soft tissue of my shoulder. I'll

need to get to a doctor and take care of this
bullet wound.

218

CHAPTER 38

They were not far from Zurich. Josh took Sarah to the United States Consulate where her wound was treated and bandaged. He cleared everything with the intelligence chief giving him a little extra background on the two Russians. He told him to contact Gabe Smith in Washington to fill him in on more history. The agent in charge assured Josh there would be no repercussions. Robbery on the highway was not uncommon, even in Switzerland.

They took the rest of the day off and rested at the hotel. The day had turned out far more eventful then they had expected. Tomorrow they would set in motion a conclusion to their adventure.

Sarah felt well enough in the morning, after taking a few painkillers, to accompany Josh to the bank. He spoke to a vice-president and laid out the details.

He wanted a three key safety deposit box. He would keep one; one would be given to another party and the third was to be kept by the bank's vice-president. On a specified date, two people would meet and open the deposit box together. Everything seemed in order with the bank so Josh deposited his package into the vault. He took his two keys and told Sarah to make her call to David Bar Simone.

CHAPTER 39

Simone was surprised to hear from the pair so quickly. He was even more impressed that they had taken out the two Russians. He had contacted Dzerzhinsky, who amazingly, had no idea what Simone was referring to. He was made aware of the fact that the Soviet Union had an immense windfall coming to them if they would meet in Zurich to discuss a barter agreement. The bait was taken and they all agreed to meet in Zurich at the Credit Suisse in one week's time.

Josh extended his leave and Sarah and he returned to Israel. Sarah jumped at the chance to show him areas of Israel previously not available before the '67 war.

Jerusalem was a big, first priority. Josh wanted to feel the presence of the Western Wall of Solomon's temple. The

Tower of David was another fascinating site. He and Sarah became certified tourists in the next week; visiting the Mount of Olives, the city of Hebron, where many of the Jewish patriarchs were buried. On their last day, they climbed to the top of Masada, where so many Jews died, rather than be enslaved by the Romans.

The day came to return to Zurich. Sarah called David Bar Simone and they all agreed to fly together to meet with the Soviet representative, Ivan Dzerzhinsky.

CHAPTER 40

The three of them proceeded to Paradeplatz and the looming structure that was Credit Suisse. The same vice-president who Josh had dealt with met them. He led them into a large conference room where they encountered the Soviet representative.

"Ivan Dzerzhinsky, at your service."

He was a short man about five and half feet. His eyes were black as coal and he looked as if he had not smiled in many years.

"I am most impressed that you accepted our invitation. I would like to introduce you to Mr. Ross and Miss Burstein, two key members of this proceedings."

"Are you Joshua Ross?"

"Yes."

"For state security reasons, you have been on our diplomatic watch list. This is not uncommon when you are a high profile diplomat."

"I would not classify myself as a high profile diplomat. Perhaps you have me confused with some other government official you have been watching."

David Bar Simone interrupted the friendly banter.

"Can we get to the purpose of our meeting, please?"

"By all means, please proceed."

Josh pressed a buzzer which called the vice-president back into the room. He handed him his key and asked him to bring the safety deposit box to the room. A few minutes later, he returned with the box. Josh opened the box and removed the Russian Battle flag and its contents. He opened them both slowly watching Dzerzhinsky out of the corner of his eye for his reaction. Once again, the jewels lit up the room with their brilliance.

The room was deathly quiet. Dzerzhinsky's black eyes lit up with astonishment as he stared, mesmerized at the necklace.

"Is this what I think it is?" he blurted, finally able to find his voice.

"It is the coronation necklace given by Peter the Great to Catherine," said Josh.

"How did you come to possess a treasure that belongs to the Soviet people?"

"It is a very long story which I do not want to get into just now. However, I am the rightful guardian of this treasure, with certain responsibilities. Alexandra, wife of Nicholas II, entrusted this necklace to my grandfather, Field Marshal Yeshica Rosofsky to help save the Russian people. It is my intention to do just that."

Dzerzhinsky looked amused, "Marshal Rosofsky was your grandfather, Mr. Ross? It is embarrassing that our people didn't make this connection" he said.

Josh leaned back in his chair, turning to smile at Sarah.

"I am all in favor of saving Russian people," said Dzerzhinsky. "How do we begin?"

David Bar Simone who had been relatively quiet, until now, spoke up with a vengeance.

"We are talking about saving Russian Jews who have been denied their right to leave the U.S.S.R and settle in Israel, their ancestral homeland."

"Please, do not be so hostile. We have treated the Jews well since the Revolution. They are all citizens of the Soviet Republic."

"Do you call the institutions of pogroms, the deportation of hundreds of thousands to Siberia, and the denial of exit visas, preferred treatment," replied Sarah.

"Please accept my apology. I do not make policy. That is the Kremlin's prerogative."

"Let's not play this game, Mr. Dzerzhinsky. What can you offer Mr. Ross for the safe return of this treasure to the Soviet people?"

"I can give you my solemn oath that I will do my best to see that the Russian Jews who wish to leave are granted visas."

"That is not good enough," replied Josh, stating his terms.

"When a minimum of 100,000 Jews are given exit visas and physically arrive in Israel, I will return the necklace to you. Not one day sooner," said Josh.

"That is a tall order. Do you realize the cost of moving so many people?"

"Not to worry. You pay for the ink and visa paper. Israel will cover the transportation costs."

"Once your Jews have arrived in Israel, how do I know that you will keep your word? I have not heard mention of the United States in our conversation."

"I am a citizen of the United States. I am also a Jew. You do not have to take my word as any part of this agreement. I will give you a key to a safety deposit box in this bank. When you have fulfilled your part of the bargain and the headlines of the Jerusalem Post announce the safe arrival of the 100,000 Jews, the bank vice-president will open the vault with you and deliver the necklace to you."

"That seems fairly straight forward. I would prefer that our agreement be kept secret. My government is a proud government and I would not want the world to get the wrong idea."

"You can tell the world that Karl Marx and Lenin came back from the grave and recommended this for all I care.

100,000 Jews with exit visas is my price. Take it or leave it," said Josh.

Sarah squeezed Josh's arm as he finished his last statement. Dzerzhinsky looked once more at the necklace and studied it carefully.

"How do I know this is not a fake?"

Josh spread out the necklace on the Tsar's battle flag. There was no doubt that these two articles were the genuine things.

"How many of these Battle flags have you seen in the last sixty years?"

"Is the flag part of the deal?"

Dzerzhinsky knew he was looking at a priceless flag that would bring top dollar on the international market. Nothing wrong in being paid a commission for his services.

"It is all part of the bargain," said Josh.

Dzerzhinsky extended his hand to Josh.

"We have a deal. It will take some time but I will start the movement that we have agreed upon.

Josh handed Dzerzhinsky a safety deposit key.

"When the headlines announce to the world of the 100,000th Jew arriving in Israel, the necklace is yours.

"Before we depart," Ivan said, "there is one more thing I would like to discuss with you. Two of our agents who were assigned to follow your movements have disappeared."

"When did you last have contact with them," replied Simone.

"It was here in Zurich about ten days ago."

"It is not uncommon in our business for agents to switch sides and defect. I could read off a whole list of U.S. and British agents who have gone over to your side and I am sure you could read me off a list of Soviet agents who have defected to the West."

"Well it seems strange that I have not heard from them."

"I am sure they will turn up eventually," replied Josh.

CHAPTER 41

The time passed quickly and Lod airport was a very busy place. Planeload after planeload of Russian Jews arrived daily from the U.S.S.R. The immense joy in the air was like static electricity, affecting everyone.

Golda Meir was invited to Washington to meet with President Nixon. The Soviets were lauded as benevolent humanitarians for their actions. Israel was dizzy with planning for the resettlement of so many new people.

Josh and Sarah set the date for their wedding.

It was a small but beautiful wedding. Sarah forgot how many cousins she had. It was truly wonderful to be among so many of her family.

They said their vows and the Rabbi gave them his blessing. Toasts were coming fast and furious. Gabe and Mary were there as they had promised. The whole United States Embassy staff attended.

Sarah stood up from her seat.

"I would like to propose a toast to my own personal Moses, or should I say Joshua, who led the Jews into the Promised Land."

David Bar Simone broke out with a broad grin. It was a great toast but not entirely comprehended by many of the people in attendance.

Josh and Sarah finally escaped the festivities and luxuriated in the quiet privacy of their hotel suite. He held Sarah's hand, and looking at her thoughtfully. It had been a long journey he thought to himself. It would make a wonderful story, if it ever could be told.

EPILOGUE

That evening, Josh and Sarah were interrupted from their reverie by a knock on their door. It was Gabe Smith and he profusely apologized for the interruption.

"I have a letter for you that I was asked to hand deliver. I will say goodnight now and I wish you both the very best."

Josh looked at the envelope. It had the seal of the President of the United States. He opened it slowly and removed the letter.

He read it to Sarah:

I want to take this opportunity to wish you and Sarah my most heartfelt congratulations on your wedding. I have heard nothing but praises about you both.

In token of my appreciation and of the appreciation of the people of the United States, I am appointing you our next Ambassador to Israel.

Josh looked at Sarah. "Did you know about this?"

"I had my suspicions. It is hard to keep a secret as big as this. The Mossad knew, therefore the Prime Minister knew. Golda was so proud of what you did, she wanted to tell the world; she settled on the President of the United Sates.

Not long after that, the Soviet Government announced a fabulous new exhibit at the Hermitage in Leningrad. The coronation necklace, the present of Peter the Great to his wife Catherine had been found and was now on display for the entire world to see.

Afterword

Warning, spoiler alert! If you are reading this, then I assume you have finished the book!

Leonard's son Dan is an artist; and he graciously volunteered to design the cover of the book. I had no idea what he had in mind for the cover so, having spent time in Istanbul, I used a photograph I had taken of *Rumeli Hisari* as a placeholder until Dan delivered his final design.

When Dan sent me the final cover I was a little confused. What was I looking at? Where did the image come from?

I asked my cousin Dan, and his answer was shocking!

"It's the tallit bag." he replied.

"Whose?" I asked.

"The tallit bag that belonged to our great-grandfather."

Dan inherited it from his father, who had inherited it from our grandfather, passed down from our great-grandfather! Hand-embroidered across the top you can see his name in Hebrew: Yehoshua Rosofsky.

The real Yehoshua Rosofsky.

This is what I know about our family history:

Yehoshua Rosofsky was a Field Marshall in the Tsar's army and was killed in the Russo-Japanese war. As was common at the time, when his son (Leonard's father), arrived in America his last name was shortened — to Ross. In the 1960s, when Leonard was working for the military, he met a very old man in a white suit who had served under Marshall Rosofsky and shared with Leonard everything he could about his grandfather.

That is what I know.

Dan assures me there is nothing hidden inside the tallit bag except, of course, his tallit.

But he also suggested that we go treasure hunting sometime.

Jared Bendis

January 2018

About the Author

Deeply influenced by his experience in the military and secrets surrounding his Grandfather's involvement in the Russian army, Leonard Ross drew inspiration from life's adventures.

At 18 he joined the Armed Forces serving in Japan, and later in Turkey as a top secret courier for the United States. From the Navy and Air Force to building his own sailboat and living aboard it in Key West, Leonard was a dreamer who remarkably brought his visions to life. This novel, though fiction, is an elaboration from his life history and the creative imagination of one spirited man.

Leonard passed away in 2009.

This was his first and only novel.

Louise Ross

January 2018

www.ingramcontent.com/pod-product-compliance
Lightning Source LLC
Chambersburg PA
CBHW070449120726
47910CB00003B/981